CW00862429

Magic Molly

Book Two

Gloop

By

Trevor Forest

© copyright T.A. Belshaw 2011
© Cover artwork and illustrations copyright Marie
Fullerton 2011
Published by Dog Eared Books 2011

No part of this work may be copied or republished without
the express permission of the author.

Special thanks to Maureen Vincent-Northam for her
patience, editing skills, and unqualified support during the
creation of this book. Thanks also go to Marie Fullerton
for designing the wonderful cover and the fantastic
illustrations.
I'd also like to mention my two Springer Spaniels, Molly
and Maisie who had to put up with late dinners and a little
less attention than usual while this book was being written.

To find out more about Trevor Forest and his books, visit.
http://www.trevorforest.com

The Story So Far

On the eve of her ninth birthday, Molly Miggins goes
to the funfair with her parents and best friend, Jenny.
Molly's mother is a High Witch and her father is a
stage magician who uses real magic. They have been
booked to perform a magic act on the opening night.
The highlight of the show, a disappearing trick, goes
badly wrong and both Molly's parents vanish.
Molly meets a wizard who has been sent by the
Magic Council. He tells her that her parents have
been sent to a mysterious place called the void and
only she can rescue them. To achieve this Molly must
join the Witch's Academy a year earlier than planned.
The wizard gives Molly a scroll containing her
special task and tells her that if she doesn't succeed
only one of her parents will be returned.
When Molly and Mrs McCraggity, the housekeeper,
go to the Witch's Outfitters to buy Molly's new
uniform, Molly accidently sits on her hat and bends
the tip. Mrs McCraggity isn't convinced by Molly's
choice of a yellow tunic instead of the traditional
black. Molly catches a glimpse of her missing father
in the shop's talking mirrors but the image vanishes
before she has a chance to learn much and the mirror
refuses to display it again.
Outside the store Molly has a run-in with her arch
rival, Henrietta Havelots, the richest girl in the
school. When she hears that Molly has been accepted
by the Witch's Academy she insists that her father
gets her a place too.
Molly has an argument with a security parrot before
her nutty, absent minded Grandmother, Granny
Whitewand, gives her a special birthday spell.

Molly attends the induction ceremony at the academy with Granny Whitewand and Mrs McCraggity. When she goes on to the stage to take her witch's promise, the wizard appears and tells the audience that Molly has just twelve hours left to complete her task.

In the wand selection room Molly discovers that all the best wands have already been handed out and she is left with a small, ancient wand with a twisted tip. The wand is called Wonky and Molly forms an immediate bond with it although she finds aiming it to cast spells very difficult.

The wizard gives Molly a pocket watch and tells her to keep an eye on the time, but to her horror she sees the clock is going backwards.

At home Molly picks up the newspaper and sees a story about two ghosts appearing in mirrors at the fun fair. She is convinced that they are her mum and dad trying to get a message to her. She hitches a ride with Granny Whitewand on her battered old broomstick and they crash land onto a field near the funfair knocking over a policeman in the process.

Molly finds her way into the hall of mirrors where Wonky tells her there is a secret entrance to the void. Molly smashes a few mirrors with a blast spell and finds a hidden staircase.

In the void Molly meets the wizard again who tells her that her father is in the centre of a maze made up of thousands of mirrors. When Molly enters the maze the wizard turns out all the lights. He makes Molly's pocket watch go backwards even faster and she has a race against time to get to the centre of the maze.

When Molly reaches the centre she finds her father waiting for her but there is no sign of her mother. The wizard congratulates Molly for finding a way around all his tricks and traps and tells her that her mother is in a different part of the void. She has been captured by a jellified ghost, called Gloop. Molly is given extra spell powers and told that she now has to find a way to defeat Gloop and bring her mum home. Now read on …

Chapter One

'Molly Miggins, get out of bed this minute. You've had three wake-up calls already.'

Molly looked at her clock and decided to have five more minutes in the comfort of her bed. She had plenty of time to eat breakfast and get ready for school.

Then she remembered, today was Sunday, she didn't have to go to school.

Molly got out of bed and stepped into her slippers. She grabbed her dressing gown from the back of the chair, pulled it over her shoulders and stomped to the top of the stairs.

'It's Sunday,' she shouted.

Mrs McCraggity's head appeared at the bottom of the stair.

'It might be Sunday young lady but there's no lie in today. You're visiting Aunt Matilda, or have you forgotten?'

Molly's mood brightened. Aunt Matilda was fun; she liked the same boy bands that Molly liked. She was a little eccentric, but she made wonderful cakes.

'You also have a birthday party to attend this afternoon.'

'Don't remind me,' groaned Molly. 'Malcolm Meany.'

'You should be happy that people like you enough to invite you to a party,' said the housekeeper as she turned back to the kitchen.

'Malcolm invites everyone whether he likes them or not,' replied Molly, 'He gets more presents that way.'

Molly washed her hands and face and presented herself at the kitchen table.

'Why are we going so early?' she yawned. 'We normally don't go until lunchtime.'

'She's at the W.I. this afternoon,' said the housekeeper.

'What's the W.I?' asked Molly, not really caring what it was.

'Aunt Matilda has a Witches Institute jam making competition to judge this afternoon, but she wants to see you before you start your first term at the academy.'

Molly tapped the top of her boiled egg and removed it with a spoon then picked up a toast soldier and dipped it into the egg.

'Yum, I love egg and soldiers.'

She looked up as Mr Miggins entered the room with Granny Whitewand. He helped her to her chair by the fire before sitting at the table himself.

'Good morning, Molly,' he said as he picked up his Sunday paper.

'Morning, Dad, ' mumbled Molly.

'Morning, Mille,' called Granny Whitewand.

'It's Molly, Grandma.' said Molly, spraying crumbs all over the tablecloth.

Granny Whitewand cackled to herself. 'I used to have a cat called Molly.'

'What did you used to call her?' said Molly mischievously. Granny Whitewand always got her name wrong.

'Molly, what else?' replied the old witch with a puzzled look.

Mr Miggins put his paper down and poured tea for himself and Granny Whitewand.

'Five lumps of sugar, just how you like it,' he said.

Granny Whitewand took the mug from him, leant back in her chair and slurped the tea.

'I've been thinking about those cabinets, Molly,' said Mr Miggins. 'I want to run some tests on them to make sure they're safe before we try to get Mum back.'

'I'll help, Dad. When are we going to fire them up?' asked Molly.

'Well,' said Mr Miggins. 'I'm booked to do a magic show at the theatre in town on Thursday night. I thought we might run the finale again then and try to reverse the spell. It will take me a couple of days to dismantle the cabinets, check them and rebuild them again.'

'Thursday?' That's another four days, Dad.'

'We have to make sure everything is right, Molly,' said the magician. 'This will be the best opportunity we have to bring Mum back. We don't want take a chance on anything else going wrong do we? '

Molly agreed that they didn't.

'Would you like to come on stage to help me with the tricks? I'll need an assistant until we get Mum back.'

'Yes please!' cried Molly. 'That would be great, Dad. But won't it be difficult having to get me, you and Mum through the vanishing cabinets?'

'I'm not letting you help with the vanishing trick Molly. I can't risk losing you as well. I'm going to try to reverse the trick without anyone going into the cabinets. I've been looking through some old magic books and I think I know how to do it.'

Molly was disappointed but didn't argue. She had something in mind herself.

Granny Whitewand finished her tea and got slowly to her feet.

'Pass me your wand, Millie, I want to copy those markings on him. I might do a bit of research at the academy this week to see if I can find out anything about it.'

Molly showered, put on her new witch's clothes and went to her mother's study. Granny Whitewand and Mr Miggins looked up as she came in.

'Have you finished with Wonky? I want to show him to Aunt Matilda.'

'Almost, Millie,' said Granny Whitewand. 'Your father is just taking photographs of him. I've already copied the markings onto paper. It really is a very old wand.'

'Older than you even,' said Molly.

'Much older than me. That's why I'm so interested in it.'

'Wonky's more than fifty,' boasted Molly.

'I think he's a lot older than that, Molly,' said Mr Miggins. 'He is damaged, that twist at the end will make it very difficult for you to aim a spell properly and he looks to have been burned or scorched at some stage in his career.'

'I'll get used to him, Dad. Wonky's the best wand ever. He's probably fired some really spectacular spells in his time.'

'I'm sure he has, Molly. The thing is though, is he safe to use now? You have to be very careful, being such a junior witch.'

Mr Miggins took a last photograph and passed the wand back to Molly.

'Granny Whitewand is going into the academy library to do some research tomorrow. In the meantime don't use it, in public at least. You will be fine practicing here at home.'

'I'll be careful, Dad, we won't go getting into trouble, will we Wonky?'

Mr Miggins opened the door and walked towards his own study.

'You haven't officially had your birthday present yet, have you, Molly?'

'I did see it, Dad,' Molly admitted. 'It's the best bike ever. I can't wait to ride it.'

'I have something else for you too,' said Mr Miggins. 'A gift from your mother.'

*****

Molly followed Mr Miggins into his study, she looked for the security parrot that sometimes guarded the door but he was nowhere to be seen.

Molly wandered round the magician's study, idly picking up trinkets and bits of magic equipment while Mr Miggins made some notes about Molly's new wand.

'Won't be a moment, Molly, I just want to write this down before I forget.'

Molly decided to have another look at her new bike. As she passed a huge old mirror that took up the best part of one wall, she noticed it was becoming misty. The mist, which had a green tinge to it, became thicker until she couldn't see a reflection at all. Molly called to her father and together they watched as the fog cleared and the ghostly face of Mrs Miggins, High Witch, magician's temporary assistant, and missing mother, appeared.

The apparition smiled down at Molly for a few seconds then a soft, faint voice echoed around the room.

'Molly, you found Dad, what a clever girl you are.'

'The voice became softer as the green mist began to cloud the mirror again then Mrs Miggins' voice began to break up.

'The curtain...watch out for...Gloop's trap...'

'Curtains?' Molly was perplexed. 'What did she mean, Dad?'

Mr Miggins shook his head.

'I'm as puzzled as you, Molly. Hopefully we'll get the answer on Thursday night, when we bring your mother home with us.'

Molly grinned.

'I can't wait for that. It's not the same having an untidy room when there's no one to tell you off for it,' she said.

'Doesn't Mrs McCraggity tell you off for it?'

'She does,' replied Molly, 'but it's mixed in with all the other things she tells me off for, so it's not the same.'

Mr Miggins laughed.

'That's the first time I've ever heard anyone say they miss being told off.'

Mr Miggins scratched his head and thought for a moment.

'Right, to business,' he said with a wink. 'I have something here for you, something very special.'

He rummaged among the papers on the table, then scratched his head and checked a drawer.

'It's here somewhere,' he said. 'Now where did I put it?'

The magician checked his magic box, searched the cupboards and even looked behind the curtains before tapping the pocket of his long, star covered robe.

'Ah, here it is. You shouldn't really be receiving this for another year, but as you've taken your Witches Promise, you can have it now.'

He handed her a small blue box with gold writing on the lid. *'For Molly, not to be opened until Witches Promise Day,'* she read.

Molly opened the lid slowly. Inside was a smaller box and inside that another. She began to think she'd been given a box of empty boxes, but in the last one sat a shiny gold ring.

She slipped it on to her finger.

'It's too big,' she complained.

'Watch carefully,' said her father quietly.

The ring suddenly began to glow, as it did, it shrank until it fitted her finger perfectly.

'The ring will grow with you, Molly; it will never be too small, or too big. You will never lose it, or forget where you have put it should you remove it from your hand. It belonged to your mother, before that, Granny Whitewand. It goes back hundreds of years. It is handed down from mother to the first born daughter on Witches Promise Day. Sadly she isn't here to perform that task, so I am standing in.'

'Thanks, Dad, I'll look after it.'

'*It* will look after you, Molly, that's its purpose. Now, let's see you ride your new bike.'

Chapter Two

Molly flicked through her Learn To Spell book as she loaded her new Crypt Kickers CD onto the MP3 player. She needed a spell to impress Aunt Matilda.

Molly read through the list of spells, at the back of the book and found one that allowed her to create a mini thunderstorm inside the house.

This spell will create a mini thunderstorm, she read. *Cast the spell using the words, Tiny Storm.*

WARNING! ONLY USE THIS SPELL IN A BATHROOM OR OVER A KITCHEN SINK.

Molly thought that this was sound advice and decided to try it out in the shower later.

Further down the list she found a spell that could make a china figurine dance.

Molly had a chalk figurine of a sheepdog guarding four sheep on her table. She decided to try it out.

She pulled Wonky from her secret pocket, stuck her tongue out of the corner of her mouth and addressed the wand.

Wonky's friendly little face appeared.

'Hello, Molly Miggins,' he said. 'Are we practicing today?'

'I've got a couple of things I want to try out, Wonky,' said Molly.

She pointed the wand at the pot dog and called out, *'Dancing Statues.'*

A purple spell drifted out of Wonky and settled like a mist over Molly's bedside table. As it cleared, the sheepdog raised itself up on its back legs and danced a Scottish jig.

'We did it,' cried Molly.

As she watched, the sheep paired up and danced a waltz around the table top. Molly clapped her hands excitedly.

'This is great, Wonky.'

The sheepdog's dance began to gather pace. He spun around and clicked his heels in the air. The sheep danced on serenely.

'Slow down, stupid dog,' called Molly.

She sheepdog ignored her and began to hurl itself around the table. It crashed into the sheep sending them spinning to the ground. Molly looked on with a frown as the sheep made a dash for freedom across the bedroom floor.

The sheepdog stopped dancing and decided that there was work to be done. It leapt from the table and ran around the room barking commands at the sheep.

'Bother,' said Molly moving out of the way as the sheep hurtled past.

The dog finally pinned the sheep into a corner of the room and gradually herded them back towards the table. Unfortunately Mr Gladstone, Molly's ginger cat was lying underneath. His eyes glistened at the sight of four woolly mice running straight at him.

Mr Gladstone raised a paw and flexed his claws; the sheep spotted him, swerved past and headed for the open door, closely followed by the madly barking dog. Mr Gladstone hared after them, skidding wildly on the wooden floor as he threw himself around the door onto the landing. A few seconds later Molly heard a crash and the sound of glass breaking.

'Oh oh,' she said quietly.

Mrs McCraggity's head appeared around the edge of Molly's door.

'What in heaven's name has got into that cat? He just made me drop your mum's favourite vase.'

Mrs McCraggity bent down and picked up five small objects from the landing carpet.

'And what on earth are these doing out here?'

Molly took the ornaments from the housekeeper and placed them back on her table.

'It's quite a complicated story,' she said, slowly.

Aunt Matilda lived in a small, leafy cottage an hour's drive away. Molly passed the time playing her favourite group, the Crypt Kickers, on her MP3 player. It had the added bonus of drowning out the noise of Granny Whitewand's snoring.

Aunt Matilda waited for them at the gate, tapping her foot to a tune playing through a set of tiny headphones. She was a small woman with short blonde hair and long earrings. She was a little older than Mrs Miggins but much younger than Granny Whitewand. She wore her witch's hat at a jaunty angle and carried a large, Zeppo handbag.

Aunt Matilda took her earphones off and waved excitedly as they got out of the car. She was the sort of woman who said lots of things at once, mixing statements and questions in a jumble of words.

'Hello everyone, Molly Miggins, haven't you grown? Did you have a good trip? Any news on Miriam? Come inside, I've got the kettle on.'

They followed her down a narrow path that meandered between trees and shrubs. It opened out onto a patio with large plant pots and bird tables dotted about in equal measure.

'Come in, come in, it is lovely to see you. We don't get many visitors do we, Wilberforce?'

Aunt Matilda patted her handbag and placed it on the table.

'Who's for tea and who's for juice? Wilberforce might have some milk.'

Molly glanced at her father with a puzzled look on her face.

'Who's Wilberforce?' she whispered. 'Why is she talking to her handbag?'

Mr Miggins shrugged his shoulders and pulled out a chair for Granny Whitewand. The old witch sat down with a creak. Molly was never sure if it was the chair or Grandma's knees that made the noise.

'Tea for me, Matilda,' she croaked. 'Four sugars please, five if it's a mug.'

Aunt Matilda placed a huge teapot on the table and set out four cups and five saucers. She poured milk into the extra saucer and opened her bag.

'Help yourself,' she said. 'I'll get some cake and biscuits. Wilberforce likes a biscuit for elevenses.'

Molly nudged her father and flicked her head towards Aunt Matilda.

'Why is she talking to her bag?' she whispered, again.

Mr Miggins told her to 'shhh' and began to talk about the weather.

Aunt Matilda poured the tea and added the sugar to Molly and Granny Whitewand's cups. As she added the milk a long brown face with bright eyes and whiskers looked out of her bag.

'Here he is,' she cooed. 'This is Wilberforce.'

Molly grinned.

'That's a nice rat, Aunt Matilda, I'd like one but I don't think my cat Mr Gladstone, would. Which pet shop did you get it from?'

'I didn't get him from a pet shop my dear, I found him in the garden one day eating the corn flakes that I put out for the birds. We liked the look of each other so I brought him inside. Wilberforce loves his corn flakes.'

As if to prove the point, Aunt Matilda measured out a cup full of corn flakes and tipped them into her bag. Wilberforce sniffed the air, left his milk and darted back into the handbag.

'That'll keep him going until dinner,' she said. 'Now, tell me all about this adventure of yours in the void. Have you found any clues to Miriam's whereabouts?'

After tea they moved through to the sitting room. Aunt Matilda sat on a stool by the piano and placed her bag on the floor beside her. Molly sat in a comfortable chair by the window.

'Are you excited about the new term, Molly? Who's going to be your form tutor at the academy? I remember my first day there, it was very strict.'

'Not as strict as it was in my day,' said Granny Whitewand. 'We weren't allowed to talk so we used to pass notes around the class. There was one girl...' she tailed off, lost in thought.

'We do a lot of witchcraft lessons at our own school now, Auntie,' said Molly. 'We do academy lessons on Saturdays. I don't know who my form tutor is yet. Granny Whitewand is going to find out for me this week. It's still strict though, they have lots of rules for things you can't do. I was told off for running at the Witches Promise ceremony.'

'I'm so sorry I couldn't come to see you, Molly, I wanted to, but my car wouldn't start. Turns out Wilberforce had chewed through some of the cables. He's a rascal at times. I couldn't play my Skeleton Bones CD in the car for weeks.'

'I love Skeleton Bones,' said Molly, 'Have you got their new one, Auntie?'

'Yes, isn't it great? I like the title track best, Boneshaker.'

'I haven't got it yet,' said Molly,' I'm saving up for it.'

'You'll love it, Molly,' said Aunt Matilda, 'Dave Macabre's voice gets better every album. I could buy it for your birthday if you like?'

'Ooh, yes please.' said Molly. 'I got the new Crypt Kickers CD from Jenny on my birthday. 'It's great, I had it on in the car.'

Wilberforce popped his head out of the bag, washed his whiskers then went back to his lunch.

'Martha Merryweather,' said Granny Whitewand suddenly.

'Martha Merryweather?' asked Aunt Matilda with a puzzled look.

'Ah you knew her too, did you?' said Granny Whitewand. 'I never did like her. She gave me chickenpox.'

Aunt Matilda stood up.

'I was going to get the Crypt Kickers album from the supermarket this week but I forgot all about it. They're open until four. Shall we go and buy it Molly? We could get your present at the same time.'

Aunt Matilda snatched up her bag and after a long search, retrieved her car keys from the fridge.

'Don't ask, Molly, I really don't know how they got in there,' she said.

Molly climbed into the front seat of Aunt Matilda's ancient old car. She had never been in it before. Aunt Matilda put her key in the ignition. The engine struggled into life at the fifth attempt.

'Yes,' she shouted happily, 'we won't need the breakdown services today.'

She plugged her portable CD player into the car's cigarette lighter, pushed a cable into the headphone socket that connected two large speakers on the rear seat, and turned the volume right up. The Skeleton Bones bleared out of the speakers. Aunt Matilda nodded her head in time with the beat.

'Do the boneshaker,' she sang.

Aunt Matilda wasn't a very good driver. They had several near misses on the way to the Shop Till You Drop Megastore. Molly covered her eyes as they kangaroo-hopped along the road. The man in the car behind tooted at them and flashed his lights as he followed. Molly looked over her shoulder. She could see him waving his hands in frustration as they crawled along for a few yards before picking up speed then slowing down again. As they reached the traffic lights near the shops the old engine stalled. The man in the car behind tooted again, Aunt Matilda wound down her window and stuck out her head.

'Don't toot me, you road hog.'

The man tooted again and shouted back.

'Time you scrapped that old banger.'

Aunt Matilda opened her bag and pulled out a silver wand. She leaned out of the window and pointed it at the car behind. There was a blue flash and the toot was replaced by a noise that sounded like a whoopee cushion deflating.

'That will teach him,' she said quietly.

Aunt Matilda calmly re-started the car. The Skeleton Bones continued to sing.

Chapter Three

At the Megastore, Aunt Matilda parked the car a hundred yards away from the nearest vehicle.

'I have a bit of trouble with parking,' she admitted. 'It's best if I leave it over here.'

Molly bit her lip and politely said nothing, she was just glad to have arrived at the Megastore in one piece.

Once in the store they headed straight for the music department. There was a set of cubicles where customers could listen to tracks before they bought the album. Aunt Matilda asked for the assistant to put the *Crypt Kickers* CD on in cubicle four.

Molly and Aunt Matilda shared the set of headphones; a thin white cable ran from Molly's left ear to Aunt Matilda's right.

'Which track is best, Molly? I'll get him to play it.'

'Track two,' said Molly. 'Down, down.'

'Down, down,' shouted Aunt Matilda to the assistant.

The sound in the headphones was lowered.

'Turn it up,' yelled Aunt Matilda.

The sound level returned to normal. Aunt Matilda stuck her thumb up to the assistant. He smiled thinly.

'Down Down.' shouted Aunt Matilda.

'Make your mind up lady,' muttered the assistant as he lowered the volume again.

Aunt Matilda burst from the cubicle leaving her half of the headphones swinging in the air.

'Young man,' she said firmly, 'I'm not sure what you are playing at, but kindly leave the volume alone. In fact turn it up a little.'

She returned to the cubicle.

'And please play track two,' she added.

Molly passed half of the headphone set back to Aunt Matilda.

'Ooh, it is good, Molly, you were right,' said Aunt Matilda as she wiggled her hips.

'Please don't dance,' muttered Molly under her breath.

Aunt Matilda began to dance.

'Down, down, DOWN, DOWN, DOWN,' she sang, as she waved her arms in the air.

People began to gather around the music department. Molly pulled Aunt Matilda's sleeve.

'Err, Auntie,' she said pointing at the crowd.

'Dance, Molly,' called Aunt Matilda, 'shake a leg.'

Molly didn't want to shake anything. She wished Aunt Matilda would stop shaking her bits too.

The track finished and Aunt Matilda marched up to the counter to a smattering of applause.

'I'll take that CD young man,' she gasped, 'what an exhilarating tune.'

Molly stared at the floor and prayed for a big hole to appear.

At the checkout counter Aunt Matilda opened her bag to find her purse.

'Where's Wilberforce?' she asked.

Molly didn't know.

'He was here when we came in,' said Aunt Matilda. 'Come on, Molly, we have to find him.'

Aunt Matilda looked around worriedly.

'We had better split up,' she said. 'I'll take frozen and cooked meats; see you at the Deli counter.'

Molly thought it was going to be like looking for a needle in a haystack. She looked through tinned goods then wandered down past the fish counter. There was no sign of Wilberforce in the bakery either. Suddenly she heard a scream.

'Help, there's a rat in the corn flakes.'

Molly ran for the cereal aisle and pushed her way through the crowd of women running the other way.

'Watch it, dear,' said one elderly lady, 'there's a rat in there, as big as your hat.'

Molly dodged the screaming customers and fought her way through to the corn flakes section. Wilberforce wasn't hard to find. Molly soon spotted his skinny tail sticking out of a jumbo box on the second shelf. Aunt Matilda arrived a few seconds later. She picked up the box and made her way back to the checkout.

'He's a clever boy is my Wilberforce,' she said to Molly as they walked through the shop. 'He picked a box with 50% extra free.'

The journey home was mainly uneventful. Aunt Matilda sang along to the Crypt Kickers and only stalled the car twice. A policeman did stop the traffic to allow her to get off a roundabout after they had driven round it a dozen times, but all in all is wasn't as scary a ride as Molly had feared.

Mr Miggins made tea while Molly recounted the story of Wilberforce's escape.

'I can't believe the manager banned Wilberforce from the store for life,' said Aunt Matilda. 'He loves going shopping with me. He only escaped because I forgot to top up my bag with corn flakes. He must have got peckish.'

Chapter Four

Molly walked up the Meany's drive with her Mrs
McCraggity. Malcolm was having a Harry Potter
themed party so Molly was dressed in her Witch's
uniform. Molly clutched Malcolm's present to her
chest as Mrs McCraggity rang the bell.

Mrs Meany answered the door.

'Oh hello, Molly. Hello, Mrs McCraggity,
welcome to Hogwarts.'

A boy's head, wearing a long white beard and a
wizard's hat, appeared round the door.

'Is that for me? Thanks.' A long arm reached out
and snatched the present from Molly's hands.

'Sorry about that. He's very excited,' said Mrs
Meany.

Molly thought it was just plain bad manners but
bit her lip as she was shown into the hall.

Malcolm eagerly ripped off the wrapping paper
that Molly had taken so much time over.

'Great, a Harry Potter talking book, thanks.'

Malcolm fished out a key from his pocket and
opened a small padlock on the door beneath the stairs.
He carefully placed Molly's gift inside then took a
quick look over his shoulder as he replaced the
padlock.

'Safe and sound,' he said to himself.

Mrs Meany led Mrs McCraggity into the sitting
room, then returned to the party.

'Right, children, we're going to have lots of fun
today. We have a children's entertainer arriving
shortly. For now grab yourself a can of pop and get to
know each other.'

Molly knew everyone in the room already, most
went to her school. She was trying to avoid having to

talk to Simon Snitcher, the class sneak, when the doorbell rang again. It was Henrietta Havelots, the richest girl in the school.

Molly groaned.

Henrietta breezed in like the Queen arriving at a garden party. She smiled her best 'I'm here' smile to everyone as she walked slowly into the room.

Her father's chauffeur carried her present for Malcolm. He handed it to him with a bow, then left the room.

'WOW,' said Malcolm, noticing the Zeppo logo on the outside of the bag. 'A Zeppo Zodiac original.'

Malcolm tore the bag open and pulled out a blue backpack with the famous Zeppo crest on a tiny green label.

'Mum,' he shouted, 'open the safe, I need to put something in it.'

Malcolm clutched the bag to his chest as if he were in a room full of thieves and backed away towards the sitting room. Two minutes later he appeared again, his face a picture of content.

'That's three Zeppo originals I have now,' he gloated.

'What good are they in the safe?' asked Molly. 'Don't you want to wear them?'

Malcolm was shocked.

'They'll be worth a lot of money one day if I keep them like new,' he said. 'Dad's got all his old records in there, he never played them when they were new and they're worth loads now.'

Molly didn't get it.

'I'd sooner wear something than look at it once a year,' she said.

Most of the party goers agreed with a nod and a murmur.

'It's not like you have any designer clothes to look at anyway,' said Henrietta, nastily. 'Every time I see you lately you're wearing the same thing.'

Henrietta did a twirl in her new designer dress.

Molly wasn't impressed.

'It's supposed to be a Harry Potter theme party, who have you come as, the girl selling the programs at the premiere?'

'You'll never have what I've got,' said Henrietta with a toss of her curls.

'Thank goodness for that, I don't think I want it,' replied Molly to a laugh from half the room.

Mrs Meany came back into the dining room.

'Bad news I'm afraid, children. Jasper Japes, our children's entertainer, has broken down and will be delayed. He's going to get here as soon as he can. For now, how about some parlour games? I've got presents wrapped up for musical chairs and pass the parcel. Who's for a game of Blind Man's Buff first though?'

The idea was greeted by a groan from the guests.

Mrs Meany placed a parcel on the end of a row of chairs and produced a headscarf from the sideboard.

'Who's first?'

Walter Wimp threw up his hand. Mrs Meany tied the scarf around his eyes and turned him round three times. Walter stuck his hands out in front and staggered blindly around the room while his fellow party goers stood out of reach behind the table and chairs.

The phone rang. Mrs Meany left the room to answer it.

After five minutes of fruitless searching, Walter managed to find his way behind the table. Henrietta stuck out a leg as he passed. Walter crashed to the floor and lifted the blindfold from one eye.

'Who did that?' he asked, rubbing his knee.

Simon Snitcher pointed at Henrietta.

'She did it, Walter.'

'Sneak,' said Henrietta. 'Anyway I don't care. It's boring. We had so much fun at my birthday party last night. It's a shame none of you were invited, you would have loved it.'

'I doubt it,' muttered Molly.

Henrietta walked around the table, deep in thought. Then she had an idea.

'Why don't you give us a spell?' she said to Molly. 'You're supposed to be a real witch.'

Molly shook her head.

'I don't think that's a good idea, Henrietta.'

The rest of the gathering thought it was a wonderful idea.

'Come on Molly,' said Malcolm. 'Give me a birthday spell.'

Molly thought about it for a moment then pulled Wonky from her secret pocket.

'Oh no,' said Wonky, 'not here.'

'It will be fine, Wonky,' said Molly confidently.

Wonky closed his eyes and waited.

'I could do the new spell I just learned,' said Molly, thoughtfully.

Molly looked around. There was a group of ornaments on the sideboard. She pointed Wonky at a figurine of a Japanese lady holding a parasol.

'Dancing Statues,' she called.

The spell spluttered out of Wonky and skidded across the polished surface of the sideboard before falling off the end and hitting the curved back of the chair that held the wrapped prize. From there it deflected across the table cloth and hit the birthday cake with a splat.

The chair lifted its two front legs and began to dance.

'Wow,' called Malcolm, 'that's great.'

The chair danced along the row of seats then turned and danced back to where it started. Molly began to feel a little proud of herself.

'Do a jig,' she called to the chair.

'The chair stopped suddenly.

'My present might fall off if I dance too fast,' it said woodenly.

'It's not your present,' said Malcolm Meany. 'It's mine, I'm going to win it at musical chairs, Mum promised.'

'You're not having this one,' said the chair, 'it's mine, anyone can see that.'

Molly stepped forward and tried to grab the parcel. The chair ran into the corner.

'Stop, thief,' it cried.

Molly tried to grab the package again.

'It's not yours, now give it back.'

'Shan't,' said the chair. 'It's my birthday present.'

'What could a chair possible want for its birthday?' said Molly.

'Polish,' said the chair, 'or a cushion.'

Molly grabbed the parcel but the chair held on. Molly pulled harder and the parcel was torn open. A soft toy fell to the floor.

'See,' said the chair, 'it's my cushion.'

Molly picked up the toy and handed it to Malcolm. He opened the cupboard under the stairs and stashed in inside.

The chair went into a sulk and sat in the corner of the room moaning about stolen cushions.

Mrs Meany re-entered the room.

'Are you all having fun children?'

There was a mumble of, 'yes' and 'I suppose so,' mixed in with the with the odd, 'no.'

'Let's cut the cake and have some food,' trilled Mrs Meany.

The party guests stood around the table as Mrs Meany picked up the cake knife.

'MURDER!' GET THE POLICE!' shouted the cake.

Mrs Meany was nonplussed.

'What? How?' she stuttered.

'I WANT MY MUM,' yelled the cake.

Mrs Meany put the knife down. The cake backed off along the table.

'Don't come near me,' it said, 'you cake-murderer you.'

Mrs Meany was shocked.

'That's the last time I get a cake from Savelots,' she said. 'I'll go to the bakery next time. You know what you're getting there.'

She picked up the knife and stepped forward. The cake backed off again. Malcolm tiptoed around the table until he stood behind it.

'Now, Mum!' he shouted.

The cake leapt from the table in a final bid to escape, Malcolm jumped forward to catch it but got hold of the table cloth instead, he rolled to the side dragging the cloth and everything it contained onto the floor with a huge crash.

'Oops,' said Molly.

Mrs Meany attempted to salvage what she could from the mess.

'Who started all this?' she asked with a frown. 'And why is that chair crying?'

Simon Snitcher pointed to Molly.

'She did it,' he said.

Molly opened and closed her mouth, but nothing came out.

The sitting room door opened and Mr Meany and the other parents walked into the devastation. Molly stood alone at the end of the bare table with Wonky in her hand as twenty pairs of eyes fixed on her.

'Bother,' she whispered.

Mrs McCraggity apologised for Molly and asked Mr Meany to send the bill for the food and the cost of the clean up. She took Molly's hand and marched her across the room.

'Do you have anything to say, Molly?' she said as they reached the door.

'Sorry,' said Molly.' It was an accident.'

'It's that wand,' said Henrietta. 'It's not safe.'

'I'll be contacting the academy about this,' said Mr Meany. 'I will be demanding compensation.'

Mrs McCraggity drove home in silence. When they arrived Molly was sent to her room.

'We'll discuss this in the morning, Molly.' said Mr Miggins. 'We will have to make a decision about the future of that wand.

Molly lay on her bed and pulled Wonky from her pocket.

'I'm sorry, Wonky. That was all my fault.'

'Not to worry Molly Miggins,' said Wonky sadly. 'I'm used to bad things happening.'

'I won't let them take you, Wonky,' promised Molly. 'We're a team.'

Chapter Five

Molly dressed in her witch's uniform and got her
things together for the first day back at school. She
was allowed to wear the witch's uniform if she had
witchcraft lessons during the day. On days where
there were not, she would wear her normal school
clothes.

Molly was one of only thirteen witches at her
school. Five of them were at level seven and would
be learning broomstick flying that year. Molly, being
a level one, was in the 'fresher's' class along with
Henrietta Havelots who had paid for a scholarship.

Mr Miggins gave Molly a stern lecture as they
drove to the school.

'Molly, please, please try to stay out of trouble this
term. It's a very important year for you. Knuckle
down and study hard. As the daughter of a witch you
should find a lot of the witchcraft lessons easy, so
please, just concentrate and work hard. I don't want
any reports about bad behaviour or cheekiness. Do I
make myself clear?'

Molly tapped her foot to the Crypt Kickers, she
looked up when she realised her father was moving
his lips but no sound was coming out. She pulled the
headphone from one ear.

'Sorry, Dad, missed that.'

Mr Miggins braked hard and pulled the car over to
the side of the road.

'This is exactly the point I have been trying to
make, Molly.'

'What is, Dad?' said Molly, as she began to realise
she was in trouble again.

Mr Miggins held out his hand.

'Hand it over.'

'But...'

'Now.'

Molly passed her MP3 player to her father. Mr Miggins tucked it into his jacket pocket.

'You can have it back when you've earned it, young lady.'

Mr Miggins started the car and lectured Molly on the benefits of good behaviour all the way to school.

*****

The morning went slowly. Molly's timetable showed her witchcraft class was the first lesson in the afternoon. By morning break Molly felt like she had done a whole day already.

She found it hard to concentrate in the maths lesson.

Mr Summit droned on for almost an hour. Molly did try to follow what he was saying but the lure of the clock dragged her eyes away from the blackboard every five minutes.

She was startled to hear her name called out.

'Molly Miggins, if I you had a bag of apples and you gave one to each of your classmates but gave two to Henrietta and kept three for yourself, how many apples did you have to begin with?'

'I wouldn't give Henrietta any apples,' said Molly absent-mindedly. 'I'd give two to Jenny.'

Mr Summit sighed.

'How many apples?'

'I'd need a sack, not a bag,' said Molly, 'there are twenty five of us.'

Mr Summit leant on Molly's desk.

'So your answer is a sack full?'

The class giggled.

Molly thought about it.

'How many did you say I get to keep?'

'Three.'

'Molly screwed up her eyes and concentrated.'

'Twenty six, no, twenty seven.'

Mr Summit tutted.

'Twenty nine?' asked Molly hopefully.

'Take fifty lines, Molly Miggins, I'm sure you'll be able to count those correctly. I want them on my desk by Wednesday.' I must not clock-watch in the maths lesson.'

'Bother,' said Molly.

*****

At lunchtime Molly bumped into Malcolm Meany and his friend Simon Snitcher. Simon was the playground monitor.

'My dad rang the school this morning,' said Malcolm. 'He's reported your bent wand. He's ringing the Witches Academy too. It's not safe.'

'Wonky is safe,' said Molly. 'I make the mistakes, not him.'

'My mum's ringing too,' said Simon Snitcher. 'She doesn't think it's safe either. She reckons it should be burnt.'

'Your mum wasn't there yesterday,' said Molly angrily.

'I told her all about it,' said Simon with a sneer. 'How your wand trashed the party.'

'Malcolm trashed the party,' replied Molly, 'by dragging all the food off the table.'

'We all went to the burger bar after you left, said Malcolm. 'Mum's sending your dad the bill. She reckons you're seeking attention because your mother went missing.'

Simon polished his glasses on his tie and looked around the schoolyard. He spotted a girl talking on a mobile phone.

'Mobile phones are banned,' he called. 'I'm reporting you to the head.'

Molly sat on the playground steps and ate her sandwiches alone.

'One thing's for sure,' she said to herself. 'The day can't possibly get any worse.'

*****

Molly arrived early at classroom thirteen. She was determined to make a good impression on Miss Hagg, the witchcraft teacher. Five minutes later her classmates began to file in. Molly was delighted to see Sally Slowspell, the girl she met at the Witches Promise ceremony.

'What are you doing here, Sally? I thought you were at Cauldron Road School?'

'I am,' said Sally, 'but there are only two witches in the whole school, so we've been transferred for witchcraft lessons. I'll be here every Monday afternoon and Thursday morning.'

'That's great,' said Molly, thinking her day was getting better at last.

Henrietta Havelots was the last to arrive. She breezed in wearing a Zeppo Zodiac designer witch costume. Her hat was made of felt with gold star at the front. Her black gown was covered in glitter. She walked to the front of the class and twirled around. Desdemona Dark clapped. She was always impressed by Henrietta.

Henrietta took her place at the front of the class. Molly and Sally sat on the back row.

Miss Hagg stood behind her desk and placed her hand on a thick, dusty, leather bound book. She introduced herself and welcomed Sally and Lisa Longnose to the school.

'This,' she said as she held up the old book, 'is the most important book ever written. It holds 90% of the spells known to witch kind. You will find an abridged version in your desk. The book is known as the *Witchit*.'

Molly raised the lid of her desk. Inside were two books, a thick black one with *Witchit* written on the cover in gold lettering and a red book called *The History of Witchery*.

'We'll begin the course by learning something about witch history. Please open the red book and turn to chapter one.'

Molly opened her history book and read along as the teacher spoke. She learned that many hundreds of years ago there were two witch academies. On the right bank of the river stood the Black Academy and on the left side, the White.

The black witches used dark magic. They were only really interested in themselves and how much power and wealth they could attain. The white witches used their magic to help nature and mankind. They were far more interested in helping others than gaining power for themselves. They all wore black gowns and the only way to tell them apart was a crest on their hats and one on the front of their tunics.

Both academies prospered, but then the white witches began to dominate. More mothers sent their daughters to the White Academy than the Black. Jealousy set in and what were once small rivalries became much larger conflicts. The Great Witch of the Black Academy hatched a plot to kidnap the leaders of the White Academy. The plot was discovered and war broke out between the two.

It lasted two years and both sides took heavy casualties. Then it was decided that too many witches were being injured and the best idea would be for the two Great Witches to battle it out among themselves in a twenty four hour spell cast.

Griselda of the White Academy with her wand, Cedron, faced off against Morgana and her wand, Bild, in the town square on Halloween. The whole population turned out to watch. The Witches stood on stone plinths and were very evenly matched. Spell after spell was cast in an effort to gain the upper hand. The wands became hot and charred as both were almost burned out of magic.

With ten minutes to go it looked like petering out into a draw. Then, Morgana pulled a hidden wand from her sleeve and began to fire fresh magic at Griselda. She was knocked from her plinth by a *Tornado* spell which picked her up and threw her violently to the ground. As she lay wounded she looked up to see Morgana waving her fresh wand in the air to proclaim victory. Griselda raised Cedron and with his last ounce of strength they cast the *Fire Dragon* spell. Morgana was picked up in a blaze of flame and dumped unceremoniously in the river. She was never seen or heard of again.

Cedron was damaged beyond repair. He was charred and twisted and could no longer cast the simplest of spells. The White witches built a large glass cabinet in the entrance hall of the academy and placed his charred remains inside for all future generations of witches to admire.

The Black Academy was cast into another dimension. Legend has it that they sometimes break free to cause trouble, especially on the night of Halloween.

Molly was entranced by the story. She had heard it before from her mother and Granny Whitewand, but now she was reading about it in the academy where the story first began. She closed her book and leant back in her chair.

'Wow,' she said aloud. 'Wouldn't you just love to have seen that?'

There was a knock on the door and a year three witch came into the room.

'There's someone to see you, Miss Hagg.'

'Tell them I'll be there shortly. Right, girls, I will be no longer than five minutes. While I'm away I want you all to think about what you've just read. I'll be asking questions when I return.'

Once the teacher had left the room the young witches began to discuss the story. Molly was really proud of the academy and its history.

'Reading that really brings it home just how lucky we are to be here.'

Henrietta disagreed.

'I can't see why everyone thinks the Black Academy was so awful. What is so wrong about having money and power?'

Molly rolled her eyes.

'Only you would think that way, Henrietta.'

'I do too,' said Desdemona, who always agreed with Henrietta.

'You'll never make a witch with that attitude,' replied Molly.

Henrietta stuck her head in her desk. A minute later she faced the back of the class with the *Witchit* in one hand and her designer Zeppo wand in the other.

'We'll see about that,' she said. Let's see who has the most skill, me and my Zeppo or you and that wonky wand of yours. We'll have our own spell cast.'

Molly remained seated.

'Here's one, so easy even you should be able to do it.'

Henrietta addressed her wand. A thin face with a top hat appeared.

Henrietta pointed her wand at the blackboard and read from the book.

'The Sunspot Spell: Create bright red sunspots on any surface, the spots will glow for ten minutes before slowly fading.'

Henrietta turned to Molly.

'Ready?'

Molly remained silent.

'*Sunspots*,' Henrietta called.

The Zeppo wand flashed bright red and exploded in her hand. As the wand crumpled its two gold tips fell to the floor. Molly collapsed in a heap.

Henrietta was incandescent with rage.

'My dad will sue the academy for this, they're obviously selling fakes.' She turned to Molly, 'let's see you do better with that tatty old relic.'

'Don't bother,' said Sally, 'she's not worth it.'

Henrietta made chicken noises and flapped her arms.

Molly stood, pulled Wonky from her pocket, then thought better of it and sat down again.

'Cluck cluck,' said Henrietta.

Molly stared at her desk.

'Cluck cluck,' said Henrietta and Desdemona together.

Molly got to her feet and addressed Wonky. His little fat face appeared on the wand.

'Not again?' he said.

Molly ignored him and pointed the wand at the blackboard.

'*Sunspots*,' she called.

A red spell flew out of Wonky and crashed into the blackboard duster, the duster flew up in the air as the spell bounced off and hit Henrietta clean in the face.

'Mmmmmf.'

'Oops,' said Molly quietly.

Henrietta took her hands from her face. Desdemona gasped.

'Oh my.'

Henrietta pulled out a gold cased mirror from her bag; she peered into it and screamed. Her face was covered in bright red spots. Some of them had developed large yellow heads.

'What have you done?' screamed Henrietta, as a huge spot burst spraying her mirror with yellow gunk.

A second spot burst with a pop. Desdemona's hat was speckled in yellow. Henrietta ran from the room with her head in her hands.

Miss Hagg returned with a puzzled look.

'Whatever is the matter with Henrietta?' She knelt, picked up the bits of wand and looked around the class. 'What's been going on here?'

Molly slipped Wonky into her secret pocket as Desdemona pointed at her.

'Bother,' she said.

Chapter Six

There was a tap on the classroom door.

'Come,' called Miss Hagg.

A year three witch passed her a note.

'Molly Miggins, you are to make your way to the headmistress's office immediately.'

'Bother,' said Molly.

'Good luck,' said Sally.

Molly made her way down the corridor and climbed two flights of stars. She knew the way, she'd been there before. She tapped on the head's door nervously.

'Enter,' said a stern voice.

Molly stepped into the office and stood in front of the head teacher's desk. Mrs Brandish was a portly woman with grey hair. She looked over her spectacles at Molly.

'Molly Miggins, Molly Miggins, Molly Miggins. That's all I've heard today. We've only been back at school for one morning and I've received two telephone calls and a bad behaviour report before lunchtime. Now I have yet another matter to deal with. What's got into you, girl?'

'There's a simple explanation,' said Molly. 'For some of it,' she added.

'I doubt it,' said Mrs Brandish. She held Molly's file in front of her.

'You've been in this office before, Miss Miggins, haven't you?'

'Yes,' said Molly, 'but...'

'I have a report here about Mrs Blast, the chemistry teacher suffering a bruised bottom after slipping on an ice slide in the playground. An ice slide made by you?'

'Yes, but...'

'Another report about a broken window, a window broken by you, with a rounder's ball.'

'Ah, but that...'

'Then there was that incident with the stink bomb.'

'Err...'

'Now I find you've caused a fellow pupil to be plagued with a face full of erupting blackheads.'

'They were supposed to be sunspots,' said Molly, 'and...'

'This isn't good enough, Molly.'

'But...'

'The latest round of reports all seem to centre on that wand of yours. Wonky, is it?'

'Yes, ' said Molly, 'but it's not his fault.'

'So, are you saying the incidents concerned were deliberate, that you meant these dreadful things to occur?'

'No, of course not,' replied Molly, 'they just sort of happened.'

'Well there won't be any more incidents of this nature, Molly. I've been on the phone to the Witches Academy and from today onwards, Wonky is banned from these premises.'

'That's not fair,' cried Molly.

'The Academy is to hold an inquiry into these incidents. They have had complaints, too. The High Witch will contact your parents shortly. I would be very surprised if you were allowed to keep such a dangerous item.'

Molly was devastated.

'Give me the wand. You can pick it up again at three thirty. But unless the academy decides otherwise, you are never to bring the wand into school again. Do I make myself clear?'

'It's not fair,' repeated Molly, 'Henrietta started it.'

'Don't try to get out if it by blaming others, Molly Miggins. Now hand over that wand.'

Molly went back to her class via the toilets. She splashed water onto her red eyes. She didn't want to let anyone else know she was upset. Henrietta was back in class, her face spot free. She smirked as Molly re-entered the classroom.

'Lost something?' she asked.

Molly ignored her and returned to her seat. Miss Hagg pointed to the blackboard and told Molly to take notes.

'What happened?' asked Sally.

'She took Wonky. He's banned from school,' whispered Molly.

'I wondered what Henrietta was looking so smug about when she came back.'

'There's going to be an inquiry at the academy. Sally, they want to take Wonky away.'

'That's so unfair,' said Sally, 'What are you going to do?'

'Fight for Wonky,' said Molly firmly. 'I'm not going to give him up.'

*****

Molly picked up Wonky on the stroke of three thirty.

'Don't worry, Wonky,' she whispered as she pushed the wand into her secret pocket. 'I'll never give you up.'

Mrs Meany and Mrs Snitcher were waiting outside the head's office as Molly came out.

'Have they burned it yet?' said Mrs Snitcher.

'No,' said Molly, 'all charges were dropped actually.'

Mrs Meany almost choked.

'What!' She spluttered. 'We'll see about that.'

Mrs Meany stormed into the head's office closely followed by Mrs Snitcher.

'That girl...' said Mrs Snitcher as she pointed to the open door.

Molly tiptoed away.

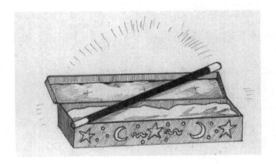

Chapter Seven

Molly caught the bus home and went straight to her
room. She knew her father was going to be furious
with her, especially after the conversation they had
had that morning. Molly set about writing out her
lines while she waited for the inevitable summons.
She was surprised to hear the whiny voice of
Henrietta Havelots floating up the stairs.

Molly crept to the landing and listened intently.
'Hello, Mrs Havelots,' said Mrs McCraggity. 'This
is a pleasant surprise.'
'Is it?' said Mrs Havelots, 'It isn't meant to be.'
Henrietta had her say.
'Molly attacked me at school today.'
Mrs McCraggity was shocked.
'I'm sure there has been a misunderstanding,' said
the housekeeper. 'Mr Miggins is in his study, just
along the passage.'
Mrs Havelots marched down the passageway
followed by a grinning Henrietta.
'Halt who goes there?' squawked a voice.
Mrs Havelots looked to the side of the door. A
colourful parrot sat on a perch staring at them.
'I'm not having a conversation with a parrot,'
announced Mrs Havelots.
'The security parrot, if you don't mind,' said the
parrot.
'I don't care if you're the King of Parrots,' said Mrs
Havelots, 'we're going in.'
'Are not,' said the parrot. 'Not without a signed
pass.'
'Don't be ridiculous,' said Mrs Havelots, 'we're
here to see Mr Miggins on a very serious matter.'
'About his daughter is it?' asked the parrot.

'Actually it is. She's a menace.'

'She is,' nodded the parrot. 'She's trouble, that one.'

Mrs Havelots tapped her foot.

'So, are we allowed in?'

'Not without a signed pass,' said the parrot. 'Unless you know the password.'

'How would we know the password, you feathered fool,' said Mrs Havelots angrily.

'You aren't doing yourself any favours here,' said the parrot.

Henrietta stepped forward.

'Stupid bird,' she said, as she grabbed the door handle.

The parrot flew from its perch and settled on Henrietta's head. It scrabbled it's feet and flapped its wings furiously. Within seconds Henrietta's immaculate curls were transformed into a something resembling a pile of old straw.

Henrietta screamed. The parrot returned to its perch.

Mr Miggins came to the door to see what the fuss was about.

'Hello, Hortense, hello Henrietta, what can I do for you? Please, step inside.'

Mr Miggins looked at Henrietta's tattered hair with a puzzled look.

'Has it turned windy? It was fine earlier.'

'We are here to complain about the behaviour of your daughter,' said Mrs Havelots, 'and your parrot,' she added.

'Parrot? We don't have a parrot. I used to have one, but it died years ago. He was a funny old thing. He used to think he was a security guard.'

'He still does,' replied Henrietta. 'He attacked me, just like Molly did.'

Mr Miggins opened the door and looked into the passage.

'No parrot,' he said.

Mrs Havelots followed him out of the room.

'It was here, what have you done with it? Magicked it away, I imagine.'

'I assure you I do not have a parrot,' said Mr Miggins firmly. 'I am a magician, but I certainly haven't been practicing magic today, especially on parrots. Now, what's this about Molly attacking you? I really do think there has been a mistake.'

'There was no mistake about it, Molly fired a spell at Henrietta and caused her beautiful little face to be covered in BOILS!'

'Boils?'

'Boils,' repeated Mrs Havelots. 'Boils that popped by themselves.'

'Yellow boils,' added Henrietta.

'If this is true then I will deal with it most severely,' said the magician, 'but I can't believe Molly would do that deliberately.'

'It's that wand of hers,' said Henrietta, 'she can't control it.'

'I know Molly must be missing her mother, but her behaviour is unacceptable. I warn you, Mr Miggins, if that wand isn't sent to the incinerator by tomorrow, you will be hearing from our solicitors.'

Mrs Havelots opened the door for Henrietta then stepped out herself. She slammed the door noisily behind her.

'Keep the noise down,' squawked a voice. 'Some of us are trying to sleep.'

*****

Molly had tea with Mrs McCraggity and Granny Whitewand while Molly's father discussed the day's events on the telephone with the headmistress.

Mrs McCraggity tutted a lot and kept saying things like, 'I don't know,' and 'whatever next?'

Granny Whitewand was more sympathetic.

'Got her in the kisser with a zit bomb, did you? Well done.'

'It wasn't like that, Grandma,' said Molly. 'She challenged me to a spell cast and it went a bit wrong.'

'Serves her right for being so uppity,' said Granny Whitewand. 'Did she really say there was nothing wrong with the Black Academy? She shouldn't be allowed in witchcraft lessons.'

'She did,' said Molly, 'but she never thinks things through properly before she opens her mouth, that's Henrietta's problem.'

'Never did like her,' said Granny Whitewand. 'How long did she have the exploding spots for?'

'Thirty minutes, that's all.' said Molly.

Granny Whitewand cackled.

'Not long enough, it should have been at least a week.'

The old witch straightened up in her chair. There was a loud crack.

'Wish I could have been there. It reminds me of the time I sent Gloria Goose a donkey ears spell in the post. That lasted for a fortnight.'

Molly stifled a laugh as she caught Mrs McCraggity's disapproving eye.

'She wasn't the belle of the ball at the Halloween dance I can tell you. She wrapped her ears up and tried to hide them under her hat.'

The old witch laughed at the memory. 'Happy days,' she said.

Mr Miggins came through to the kitchen.

'Molly, would you come to my study please? We need to talk.'

Molly's stomach churned. She knew what was coming.

For the second time that day Molly found herself standing before a large desk, this time it was her father wearing a disapproving face.

'Wonky,' said Mr Miggins.

'What about him?' said Molly. 'None of this was his fault.'

'I understand you have a problem aiming the wand, Molly, that's the reason I told you not to use it outside of this house. Do you remember that conversation? It was only yesterday morning.'

'Yes, Dad,' said Molly.

'Then why did you disobey me, Molly? I'm very disappointed in you.'

'I didn't deliberately disobey you,' said Molly, 'Henrietta challenged me. She was trying to make me look silly.'

'And yesterday?'

'Malcolm asked for a spell for his birthday, but I suppose I was showing off really.'

'I'm glad to hear you admit it, Molly.' said Mr Miggins. 'We all know what Henrietta is like, but the fact remains, Wonky, in his present condition, is not safe to use.'

Molly stuck out her jaw. 'I'm not giving him back, they'll put him in a museum,' said Molly.

'If you mean the academy then I think you'll find that being put in a museum is at the lower end of what is being demanded. There are people who want Wonky destroyed, Molly.'

Molly felt tears well up in her eyes. 'Mrs Snitcher, no doubt. She wasn't even there, Dad, and Mrs Meany only cares about how much compensation she can get out of it.'

'I do sympathise, Molly, but at the moment there is very little we can do. We'll have to wait for the inquiry. Granny Whitewand will give evidence if she finishes her research in time.'

Mr Miggins stood up and walked around to the front of the desk.

'You're grounded, Molly, until further notice.'

Molly looked at her feet. 'Sorry, Dad, I didn't mean any harm.'

Mr Miggins expression softened.

'Research can turn up all sorts of unexpected things. Keep your chin up.'

He opened the door to let Molly out.

'I do believe that Mrs Havelots is seeing things. She is convinced that I own a security parrot. I used to, but it died before you were born.'

Molly opened her mouth, then closed it again. She had seen the parrot herself, on more than one occasion. She looked at the father's laughing face and decided not to mention it, for now.

Chapter Eight

At eight o'clock Molly decided to have a bath. She usually had a shower but thought that a nice long soak might ease away some of the cares of the day. She put in some green bubble bath and floated a plastic duck and a toy boat on the water.

Molly looked through her *Learn To Spell* book as she ran the bath. Her eyes were again drawn to the *Tiny Storm* spell.

Molly fired up Wonky.

'Won't you get into trouble again, Molly Miggins?' he asked.

'Dad said it's all right to use you in the house, it's outside that's the problem.'

Wonky looked uncertain.

When the bath was three quarters full, Molly turned off the taps and pointed Wonky at the ceiling above the foamy water.

'Tiny Storm,' she called.

Wonky flashed bright yellow and a small cloud began to float in the air above the bath.

'That's cute,' said Molly,' let's have another one.'

Before Wonky could protest Molly fired another spell.

'Tiny Storm,' she called again.

A second cloud drifted alongside the first.

'Not much of a storm,' said Molly, 'one more.'

Once again Wonky flashed yellow and a third cloud appeared. They began to bump into each other to form one larger cloud. The cloud quickly expanded until it covered an area the size of the bath. Suddenly there was a loud clap of thunder.

'Oops, ' said Molly.

A fork of lightning lit up the room.

'Oh oh,' said Molly, beginning to worry.

A small wave began to form under the taps. By the time it hit the far end it had doubled in size. The water became choppy, then a violent wave ran across the whole length of the bath, the boat and duck were tossed into the air; thunder boomed around the bathroom as one lightning flash after another filled the air.

Molly began to panic. She looked to the back of the book and searched desperately for a reversing spell but there were none to be found.

'What are we going to do, Wonky?' Molly shouted.

A fork of lightning hit the metal tap and bounced straight up into the light bulb, there was a bright flash and a loud *plink* then everything went quiet...and dark.

Molly heard Mr Miggins call from downstairs.

'Don't worry, Molly. It looks like we've blown a fuse. I'll see to it. What are you doing up there? It sounds like a herd of elephants are charging around.'

Molly pushed Wonky into her secret pocket, sat on the bath stool and waited for the lights to come back on.

*****

After her bath Molly sat in front of the computer and gathered all the facts she needed to complete her homework project. She decided Mr Summit's lines could wait until tomorrow. They didn't have to be handed in until Wednesday.

Molly checked her new academy email address. There were three unread messages.

The first was a general 'Welcome to the Academy' email. It gave lists of teachers, and had a plan of the classrooms. There was also a list of rules.

Molly decided to read it later and opened the second email. It was from Sally Slowspell.

Hi Molly. I hope you didn't get into too much trouble at home. Do you think you could come to my house for a sleep-over this weekend? Mum says it's fine with her if your Dad will agree.

I'm still laughing at Henrietta's exploding spots. Thank you so much for that, sorry you got into trouble. Hope your mum comes home soon.

See you on Thursday morning.

Sally.

Molly replied.

Hi Sally. Won't be able to sleep over as I'm grounded until further notice. Henrietta's mum is threatening to take Dad to court and Mrs Snitcher wants to have Wonky destroyed.

I'll hide him if I have to, they aren't going to take him away to some stuffy old museum.

I made a storm in the bath tub tonight. It went a bit wrong, but it's all sorted out now.

See you on Thursday.

Molly.

Molly read the third email through gritted teeth.

Hello poor witch. Prepare to lose you precious wand. Dad has been told that the academy is going to destroy it.

Ha Ha.

I wonder what they'll give you as a replacement? Something plastic probably.

My dad is buying me the latest Zeppo wand tomorrow, it can fire a spell for two hundred yards and has a laser guiding system built in. Oh yes, it has diamond encrusted tips as well.

Want to take up the challenge again? Be careful, they might expel you next time.

Dad made a generous donation to the school by the way. He was thinking of letting me go to a private school, but he likes me to see how the other half live.

He says he won't take your father to court as you have no money, so it's not worth it.

Yours pityingly.

Henrietta.

Molly turned off the computer and got into bed. She closed her eyes and conjured up an image of Henrietta with her face covered in spots. She smiled at the memory and drifted off into a happy sleep.

The next day Molly went to school determined to concentrate on her lessons. There was no witchcraft class so she wore her normal school uniform. All went well in the first lesson, English. Molly sorted out her verbs and adverbs and scored well on her quiz sheet.

At morning break Molly talked to her best friend, Jenny, as she drank her juice.

'When do you hear from the academy about the inquiry?' Jenny asked.

'Today I suppose. I've been trying not to think about it but it keeps popping into my mind.'

'They have to let you keep Wonky. It really isn't fair. Everyone knows Malcolm's mum is just out for what she can get.'

'So is Mrs Snitcher,' replied Molly with a frown. 'Henrietta is doing her best to stir things up too.'

'Oh her!' said Jenny, 'Her mum rang my mum last night to ask if we had any complaints about you or your wand.'

'It's a conspiracy,' said Molly. 'But I won't give him up.'

Malcolm Meany wandered across to the girls. Simon Snitcher followed, determined not to miss any gossip.

'My mum's got an appointment at the academy this morning. She's seeing the High Witch,' said Malcolm.

'So is my mum,' said Simon.

'Good for them,' said Molly. 'I've seen her a few times already, she's nothing special.'

'She's handing in a written complaint,' said Malcolm.

'So is my mum, ' added Simon.

Molly rolled her eyes skyward.

'Malcolm and his parrot,' she teased.

Jenny laughed.

'Who's a pretty boy then?' she squawked.

'Polly want seed?' said Molly.

'Bullying the playground monitor is against the rules,' said Simon Snitcher. 'I'm going to report you both.'

Molly and Jenny giggled as they ran to the next lesson.

Molly did her best to concentrate in the Geography lesson. The teacher, Miss Place, loaded a map of Europe onto the projector. She asked questions as she pointed with a long stick.

'Jenny, what country is this?'

'Germany, Miss?'

'Are you asking me or telling me, Jenny?'

'Telling, Miss, it's Germany.'

'Henrietta, what is the name of this country?'

'That's easy, Miss, it's Italy, I went to Milan to buy clothes with my mum. We stayed at the...'

Molly's mind began to drift as Henrietta waffled on about designer clothes and Italian hotels. She began to think about the inquiry. What could she say to help save Wonky? None of her excuses seemed good enough.

'Molly Miggins, what is the capital of France?'

'Molly Miggins?'

Miss Place bought her stick down on Molly's desk with a crack.

Molly jumped.

'The capital of France is?'

'F,' said Molly confidently.

The class erupted into laughter. Miss Place walked to the back of the class and turned off the projector.

'Take a hundred lines, Molly Miggins. I must concentrate in the geography lesson. Have them on my desk by tomorrow.'

'Bother,' whispered Molly.'

*****

At lunch Simon Snitcher informed Molly and Jenny that they had to go and see their form teacher.

'Bullying will not be tolerated at this school,' she said.

'We weren't bullying,' said Jenny, 'we only called him a parrot.'

'A parrot?'

'Because he always repeats what Malcolm says,' Molly explained.

'So, you called him a parrot, then what happened?'

'Nothing,' said Molly,' we just ran off.'

'You ran off?'

'Yes,' agreed Jenny.

'Hmm, ' said the teacher, 'bullying does seem a little strong a description.'

She thought for a moment.

'Both of you get fifty lines.'

'That's so unfair,' said Jenny. 'Fifty lines is a lot for calling someone a parrot.'

'It's not for the name calling,' the teacher informed them.' It's for running on the school premises.'

Chapter Nine

When Molly got home her father was waiting at the door.

'We have to go to a meeting at the academy tomorrow morning, Molly. The committee heard the evidence from the complainants this afternoon. You have the chance to tell your side of the story now. The school has been informed and they are not expecting you to attend tomorrow.'

Molly went up to her room to do her homework. Then she remembered the lines.

'Bother, bother, bother, two hundred lines.'

Molly sat on the edge of her bed and put her chin in her hands. How was she going to do the homework and all those lines in one evening? It was impossible.

Then she remembered something she had read in her Learn To Spell book. She flicked through the pages until she found the *quill* spell.

The Quill Spell.

This spell will produce a quill pen. The pen will write to command.

Uses. The spell is handy when a junior witch needs to write a letter, possibly to an Aunt who sent a birthday present.

To summon, address the wand, call, 'The Quill' then dictate.

'That's the very spell I need,' said Molly.

Molly placed a single sheet of paper on her table then set the rest of the stack alongside it. She pulled Wonky from her secret pocket and addressed him.

'Hello, Molly Miggins, are we practicing again?'

'Not this time, Wonky, we have urgent business.'

Molly aimed Wonky at the table.

'The Quill,' she called.

A light blue spell drifted lazily from Wonky, a quill pen appeared above the paper on the table.

'Quill, please write, fifty times, I must not clock-watch in the maths lesson.'

The quill began to write in a beautiful flowing script. At the end of the page it stopped and waited as a new sheet floated to the table from the stack.

'This is great,' said Molly.

She picked up her Creepy Tales comic from the floor, lay on her tummy and began to read.

After half an hour the quill had only done thirty lines, the writing was beautiful but there were only six lines to a page. Molly thought about trying to speed up the process. She opened the spell book again.

The Swift spell, she read.

This spell will speed up a routine process.

Uses. This spell is useful when used in tandem with another spell. For instance, combined with the washing up spell it will speed up the process, causing the dishes to be washed much more quickly.'

To summon, address the wand, call, Swift...and then the action you wish to carry out.

Molly addressed Wonky again and pointed him at the quill.

'Swift, Quill,' she called.

The quill began to write faster, it flew across the pages, within two minutes the fifty lines were complete.

Molly was delighted.

She pointed Wonky at the quill again.

'Swift Quill, please write, I must concentrate in the geography lesson, one hundred times.'

The quill got to work and fifteen minutes later the lines were complete.

Molly was really impressed. She lay back on her bed and called out.

'Swift, Quill, I must not run on the school premises.'

As the quill began the lines, Molly decided to get herself a drink of orange juice from the fridge. Mrs McCraggity was in the kitchen making a pie for dinner the next day.

'Good luck with the inquiry tomorrow, Molly,' she said. 'I hope it all goes well.'

'Thanks,' said Molly. 'I'm really nervous about it. What if they take Wonky away?'

Mrs McCraggity sympathised.

'It's a pity your mum isn't here, Molly, 'I'm sure she could talk them round. She's a wand expert.'

'Mum won't be back before Thursday night at the earliest,' said Molly. It might be too late by then.'

Mrs McCraggity patted Molly's hand.

'It will work out alright in the end, dear, I'm sure of it.' She looked at her watch. 'Goodness, is that the time, I'd better get this pie in the oven. Shouldn't you be doing your lines, Molly?'

'MY LINES!' cried Molly, ' I forgot all about them, I didn't tell the quill how many to do.'

Molly raced from the kitchen and took the stairs two at a time. She pushed the bedroom door and ran inside.

'Bother,' she said, as she looked around.

The Quill had finished the lines but because Molly hadn't set a limit, it had carried on writing. Molly's walls, bedclothes, pillow and carpet were covered in ink. The quill was still busy, writing the lines on the curtains.

'At least the ceiling is clean,' said Molly.

As if under command the quill left the curtains and began to write on the ceiling above Molly's bed. Molly climbed onto the bed and bounced as high as she could, flailing her arms madly in the air in a vain attempt to catch the quill.

'Nooooo,' called Molly. 'STOP!'

Mrs McCraggity appeared at the door.

'What the...' she spluttered.

'I can't stop it,' cried Molly. 'There's no *end* spell.'

Mrs McCraggity went to fetch Granny Whitewand. It took a good five minutes to get the old witch up the stairs. By then the quill was writing on the skirting boards.

Granny Whitewand took one look, lifted her wand and called, '*cease quill*'.

The quill stopped immediately.

'Been getting the old quill spell to do your lines have you?' she cackled.

Mrs McCraggity didn't find it so amusing. 'Someone has to clean up this mess,' she said.

'Don't be too hard on her, all witches use this spell when they're young,' said Granny Whitewand. 'The trick is to remember to set limits. I once covered an entire white cottage with lines after I fell asleep in the garden.'

Granny Whitewand raised her wand and set a *clean* spell to work. Within a few minutes the whole room was back to normal.

'Can I have that spell please, Grandma,' said Molly. 'It would come in handy when I have to tidy my room.'

'Sorry, Molly,' chuckled Granny Whitewand. 'Chores are chores, you'll just have to do them like everyone else.'

The housekeeper led Granny Whitewand back down the stairs while Molly went back to her homework. At nine o'clock she had a shower, cleaned her teeth and climbed into bed. She placed Wonky under her pillow before turning off the light.

'I'll keep you safe, Wonky,' she promised.

Chapter Ten

At 2 am Molly sat up in bed, wide awake. A low
humming noise filled the room. Molly cocked her
head to try to identify the sound; it seemed familiar
but she couldn't quite place it. The sound appeared to
be coming from her father's study, which was situated
directly beneath her room.

Molly retrieved Wonky from under her pillow and
called the *glow in the dark spell.*

'I knew that would come in useful,' she said. 'Let's
investigate.'

Molly crept down the stairs and along the
passageway. The parrot squawked out a warning as
she approached.

'Halt! Who goes there?'

'It's the Easter Bunny,' said Molly.

'You don't look like the Easter Bunny,' said the
parrot.

'That's because I'm not him,' said Molly.

'Why did you say you were then?' asked the parrot
suspiciously.

'Just let me in,' said Molly, 'I've no time for games
tonight. We've come to investigate that strange
humming noise.'

'What's the password?'

'Millet,' said Molly with a sigh.

'Wrong,' said the parrot. 'Have another go.'

'But you told me it was millet on Sunday,' said
Molly.

'That was Sunday.' said the parrot, 'it's changed
since then.'

Molly began to get angry. She looked the parrot in
the eye. 'I thought we had an agreement.' she said.

The parrot thought for a moment.

'No, can't remember.'

'An agreement, regarding my cat...'

'Oh, *that* agreement,' said the parrot. 'Why didn't you mention it before? Please go in.'

Molly opened the door to her father's study and crept inside. At the far end of the room, the vanishing cabinet was pulsing with a green light. The humming noise got louder as Molly approached.

'Something's not right here, Wonky.'

'Do you think we should get Mr Miggins?' asked Wonky.

'In a minute,' said Molly. 'I just want a look inside first.'

As Molly opened the cabinet door, the humming got louder. She stepped inside and closed the door behind her.

'We don't want to wake the whole house up,' she said. 'There might be nothing to report.'

The light in the cabinet was bright enough for Molly to see without the aid of Wonky, so she shut him down, walked to the back of the cabinet and placed her hand on the mirror.

'Nothing wrong here, Wonky. But something has started the cabinet up. I wonder if we can make it work this time.'

Molly concentrated hard, raised Wonky in the air and stuck her tongue out of the corner of her mouth.

'Vanish!' she called.

Molly watched the rear wall closely. Her reflection began to fade as the mirror became transparent. After a few seconds it disappeared completely to be replaced by a thin grey curtain of mist. Molly took a deep breath and stepped forward holding Wonky out in front. Suddenly the mist began to get heavier. The grey tint changed to a sickly green as it took on an almost jelly-like form. Molly pushed Wonky into the gooey mess and pushed hard. The green slime stretched as though made of elastic. Molly pushed with all her strength, but the sticky wall was too strong.

Molly peered through the thick gooey screen, in the distance she thought she could make out a faint light.

'There's something up there, Wonky. I can see a light.'

Molly narrowed her eyes and tried to look through the screen, but it was too thick to make anything out clearly.

Then she heard a low voice.

Molly placed her ear next to the green wall and listened intently. The voice reminded her of a magic show she had once seen, when a ventriloquist made the dummy talk while drinking a glass of water.

'Goodnight my friends, Gloop will watch over you while you sleep.'

'Gloop!' cried Molly. 'He's in there Wonky and if he's there, so is Mum.'

Molly threw herself against the wall and tried to tear a hole in the green goo. The film stretched but held firm.

'Bother,' she said, 'I thought we were going to make it then, Wonky. Maybe we need Dad to cast the spell from outside after all, but at least we know where this Gloop character is now.'

Molly stepped out of the cabinet and closed the door behind her. The pulsing, green light faded, then died completely. By the time Molly reached the door of the study, the humming sound had ceased too.

Molly stepped out of the study and closed the door behind her. The parrot eyed her from its perch.

'Cuttlefish,' said the parrot.

'Pardon,' said Molly.

'The password is cuttlefish. In case you come back.'

'You do know you're dead, don't you?' said Molly.

'Shhh,' hissed the parrot. 'Don't tell everyone.'

'So you do know?'

'Yes,' said the parrot sadly, 'but they don't need security parrots over there. No one steals anything and as there are no trespass laws, nothing needs guarding, so I thought I'd come back here and do my old job.'

'How come Dad can't see you?' asked Molly.

'I hide when he's about,' whispered the parrot. 'If he sees me he might send me back for good, then I'll have nothing to protect. My security skills will be wasted. Don't tell him... please.'

'Dad wouldn't do that,' said Molly. 'Not if he knew why you're haunting the lobby.'

'I can't risk it,' said the parrot. 'I'd hate to be stuck over there all the time with nothing to do.'

Molly began to feel a little sorry for the parrot.

'I won't say anything,' she promised. 'Goodnight.'

'Goodnight, Molly Miggins,' said the parrot. 'I hope you get your mum back soon. I like her, she tries to guess the password.'

Molly crept back upstairs and slipped into bed. She pushed Wonky under her pillow and fell instantly asleep.

Chapter Eleven

Mr Miggins parked the van at the academy and he
and Molly made the long walk across the quadrangle
and up a long flight of steps to the entrance hall. The
huge wooden doors opened with a long groan as they
approached. Inside the cavernous hall, the oak
panelled walls were covered with paintings of old
witches. Half a dozen broomsticks hung from thick,
ceiling beams. On a plinth at one end of the room sat
a huge, black, iron cauldron. At the centre of the hall
was an empty glass display cabinet above which,
hung an enormous sign which read, Welcome to the
Academy of Witches. Underneath, in smaller writing
was the disclaimer. Visitors enter at their own risk.

Ramona Rustbucket was waiting for them by the
display cabinet.

'Follow me,' she said, curtly.

She led them along a maze of passageways until
they came to a door marked Committee Room. Miss
Rustbucket rapped firmly on the door, waited for the
command to enter, then opened it and led Molly and
her father inside.

The High Witch was seated at a long table with
four other witches. At the side of the room Mrs
Snitcher and Mrs Meany were sat on an old leather
sofa. They glared at Molly as she entered.

The High Witch rose and picked up a piece of
paper from the table. She motioned for Molly to step
forward.

'Molly Miggins, it has come to our attention that
you have been causing trouble among the non-witch
fraternity and bringing the name of the academy into
disrepute. How do you plead?'

'Not guilty,' said Molly.

The High Witch looked down her long nose at Molly.

'This is a something of a record, I have to say, Molly Miggins. You haven't taken your first lesson at the academy yet and here you are in front of a disciplinary.'

'It's all a misunderstanding,' said Molly. 'I didn't mean to...'

'Silence,' called the High Witch. 'The accused will speak only to answer questions put to her.'

Molly bit her lip and nodded.

'It appears that most of the trouble stems from the wand you chose on Saturday at the promise ceremony. Is that correct?'

'Not really,' said Molly. 'Wonky only does what I command him to do. Things just go a bit wrong sometimes.'

'A bit wrong? I would say things go very wrong, Miss Miggins. Wouldn't you agree?'

The committee and accusers mumbled agreement. Mrs Snitcher pointed at Molly.

'You trashed a birthday party causing my son to have nightmares about murdered cakes and screaming chairs.'

'Sorry,' said Molly. 'That was an accident.'

'And was the infliction of erupting boils to the face of a fellow student an accident too?'

'Yes,' said Molly, 'I didn't aim at her, it just...'

'Now we come to the crux of the matter,' said the High Witch. 'Place Wonky on the table please, Molly.'

'I forgot to bring...'

'Now, Miss Miggins,' said the High Witch, sternly.

Molly pulled Wonky from her secret pocket and placed him on the table. The High Witch picked it up and looked down its length.

'This wand is seriously flawed,' she said. 'The twist in the end would make it almost impossible to control.'

'I'm getting better at it with practice,' said Molly. 'You just have to remember to aim a little bit to the left and...'

'Silence,' said the High Witch.

She passed the wand along the line of committee members.

'As you can see, the wand is in what could be easily be described as a dangerous condition. What are our options, Miss Rustbucket?'

Ramona Rustbucket read from the academy rule book.

1. The wand be confiscated and placed back in the wand pool until a more experienced witch is found.

2. The wand be placed in the academy museum as an exhibit.

3. The wand be destroyed in the academy incinerator.

'Burn it,' hissed Mrs Snitcher.

'I want you to agree my compensation first, but then you can burn it,' said Mrs Meany.

Tears ran down Molly's face. *This can't be happening*, she thought. She turned to her father for support.

'Dad, you can't let them burn Wonky, it isn't fair.'

Mr Miggins got to his feet.

'I have read the rules concerning faulty wands and there is another option that for some reason hasn't been mentioned.'

Mr Miggins pulled a book from his pocket, turned to a marked page and read.

'If it is possible for a damaged wand to be repaired, then it must be attempted before all other options are considered.'

'Thank you for your input, Mr Miggins,' said the High Witch grumpily.

'If my wife were here, I'm sure that she would favour that option,' the magician replied. 'We have to give Wonky every chance.'

'That's all well and good,' said the High Witch. 'But where can we send it? There are no wand repairers around anymore to my knowledge.'

'There is a very good antique renovation shop in the town.' said Mr Miggins. 'I'm sure they could straighten him out a bit.'

'Very well, ' said the High Witch. 'Take the wand to see if he can be repaired. We will reconvene this disciplinary meeting at 3 pm.'

Mrs Meany turned to the High Witch.

'I'll get a few bits of shopping in while we wait then. I can't hang around here all day.'

Mr Miggins drove the van into town and parked outside an old shop called 'Oldwoods'. A small bell tinkled as they opened the door. The shop was full of highly polished, antique furniture. A smiling man with thick spectacles stepped forward to greet them.

'Hello,' he said. 'You must be Professor Miggins and Molly. I'm Oliver Oldwood.'

'Thank you for seeing us at such short notice,' said Mr Miggins.

'It's my pleasure,' said Mr Oldwood. 'Can I see the wand?'

Molly reluctantly pulled Wonky from her secret pocket and handed it to Mr Oldwood.

'Hmmm, this is very old wood and the carvings are very intricate. I have seen a few antique wands in my time but this is probably the oldest.'

'Wonky's more than fifty,' boasted Molly.

'Much more than fifty,' agreed Mr Oldwood. 'It appears to have been charred, has it been in a fire?'

'Not to our knowledge,' said Mr Miggins. 'But Molly has only owned it for a couple of days and we know nothing of its history.'

'Well, you've come to the right place. If we can't restore it, no one can.'

Mr Oldwood led them up some steps to his workshop.

'First things first, let's see if we can get a bit of moisture into the wand. We'll try the steam cabinet.'

Mr Oldwood walked to a machine with lots of rusty old pipes and valves attached. He placed Wonky carefully inside the chamber, closed the glass cover and fixed four clamps to hold the lid in place.

'Good luck, Wonky,' whispered Molly.

Mr Oldwood pushed a large green button marked, *ON* then turned a squeaky valve to allow the steam to enter the chamber. After a couple of minutes he set the dial to *HIGH* and opened a larger valve.

The machine chugged and hissed then began to shake violently. Mr Oldwood tightened one of the valves and pulled a lever, wisps of steam seeped out from under the glass and a red light began to flash on the control panel.

'Is something wrong?' asked Molly.

'No,' said Mr Oldwood. 'We don't normally set the level so high, that's all. It will settle down in a minute or two. Now, can I offer you a cup of tea?'

The restorer led them to a small office overlooking the workshop. He plugged in a kettle and produced three cups from a cupboard.

'Sugar and milk?'

'How long will it take?' asked Molly.

'To make tea? Not long.'

'No,' said Molly impatiently. 'How long does Wonky have to stay in that cabinet. It looks awfully hot in there.'

'It's a bit like a sauna,' said Mr Oldwood. 'I think your wand might quite enjoy it.'

'I wouldn't,' said Molly. 'I don't even like it when I have a cold and Mum makes me sit with my head over a bowl of hot water.'

After tea, Mr Oldwood led them back to the workshop. He shut down the valves, pushed the lever back up and pressed a red button marked *STOP* to switch off the machine. As he removed the clamps and lifted the glass lid, a cloud of steam rose into the air. Molly rubbed her eyes then crossed her fingers.

As the steam cleared Molly stared into the machine with a horrified look on her face. The twist in the end of the wand was gone but Wonky was the shape of a banana.

'What have you done?' she cried.

'Oh dear, 'said Mr Oldwood as he lifted Wonky from the machine. I've never seen that happen before. He is a lot cleaner though.'

Molly stamped her foot and turned to her father.

'They'll never let me keep him like this, Dad. He's worse than ever.'

Mr Oldwood thought for a moment.

'Bring him over here,' he said.

Molly followed Mr Oldwood to a bench on the far side of the workshop. He opened the jaws of a large steel vice and placed Wonky between them.

'Let's try this while he's still nice and pliable after the steam.'

He turned the handle of the vice a fraction at a time, the jaws began to close and Wonky began to straighten.

Molly watched carefully as Mr Oldwood continued to turn the vice handle. Wonky began to creak alarmingly but the restorer patted Molly's hand and told her not to worry. When the jaws were almost tight together he wound the handle back to relax the grip, removed Wonky from the vice and measured him against a steel ruler.

'Not bad,' he said. 'Now for the last procedure.'

Mr Oldwood clamped one end of Wonky into the jaws of a small vice, then slid another vice along a rail and clamped the other end of the wand. He turned an old metal wheel and the clamps began to move apart stretching Wonky in the process.

Mr Oldwood produced his tape measure and calculated the distance between the vices. Satisfied, he nodded to himself and turned back to face Mr Miggins.

'More tea?' he asked.

After half an hour, which seemed like half a day to Molly, they returned to workshop. Molly waited with bated breath as Mr Oldwood turned the wheel and undid the clamps. He lifted Wonky into the air and looked down his length turning the wand between his fingers.

'There we are, straight as an arrow and clean as a whistle,' he said.

Molly was delighted. She addressed Wonky, his fat little face appeared on the wand.

'Are you all right, Wonky?'

'I'm well, thank you, Molly Miggins, though it was an uncomfortable experience. The steam cabinet was particularly unpleasant.'

'Look how beautiful you are though, Wonky. I can see all your markings now.'

'I do feel nice and clean, Molly Miggins, it was strangely refreshing.'

Molly skipped to the door of the shop with Wonky in her hands.

'They can't possibly find a fault with you now,' she whispered. 'You look like a brand new wand.'

Mr Miggins paid Mr Oldwood and thanked him for his efforts. Then he drove Molly back to the academy.

Chapter Twelve

At 3 pm Molly and Mr Miggins were allowed back
into the committee room. Molly groaned as she saw
Henrietta and her father sitting with Mrs Meany and
Mrs Snitcher.

'Well,' said the High Witch. 'What was the result?'

'He's good as new,' replied Molly. 'Better than
new probably.'

The High Witch took the wand from Molly and
studied it carefully.

'It looks to be straight,' she sniffed.

'Don't sound so disappointed,' said Molly, under
her breath.

The High Witch passed the wand to the other
committee members. When they had inspected it she
placed it on the table in front of Molly.

'I still want compensation,' said Mrs Meany.

'So do I,' said Mrs Snitcher.

Mr Miggins rose to his feet.

'I have already stated that I am willing to pay for
the damage done at the party and the cost of the clean
up. I really can't see why anything else would need to
be paid.'

Mrs Snitcher and Mrs Meany began to complain.
Mr Havelots got to his feet.

'Henrietta suffered the most in all of this,' he said.
'She had nightmares last night about the spots that
were inflicted on her.'

The High Witch nodded.

'It can't have been a very nice experience,' she
agreed. 'But, I have heard evidence that it was
Henrietta who challenged Molly to the spell cast. If
such a challenge is made and accepted, then both
contestants must accept any repercussions that may

arise as a result. Henrietta clearly issued the challenge, she must accept the consequences.'

Mr Havelots sat down with a frown. Henrietta looked at him quizzically.

'What's a reaper cushion and when do I get it?' she asked.

Molly stepped forward to pick up Wonky but the High Witch held up her hand to stop her.

'The wand may look as if it's been repaired but we need to test it before we can issue it with a licence.'

She sat down and had a whispered conversation with the other committee members. Molly put her hands behind her back and crossed her fingers. Eventually the High Witch stood up again.

'The wand must be tested on the spell casting range this afternoon. It will require an 80% success rate before we can consider issuing the licence.'

'What happens if we don't get the 80%?' asked Molly nervously.

'The wand will be sent to the incinerator to be burned. There will be no appeal.'

'Yes,' hissed Henrietta.

'It should be burned anyway,' said Mrs Snitcher.

'I'm still putting in a claim for compensation,' said Mrs Meany. 'The academy issued the wand, so they have to pay something.'

The High Witch gave Mrs Meany a withering look.

'Just a token amount?' asked Mrs Meany, desperately.

The High Witch thought for a moment.

'It seems to me that there is no case to be made. Your son, Malcolm, asked an academy pupil to perform a spell at a public gathering. The fact that the spell went wrong is neither here nor there. As she is such an inexperienced witch, there is an argument that even with a different wand the outcome could have been the same. Therefore, as an offer of compensation has been made by the parent of the pupil, the matter is closed. The academy's responsibility lies in making sure the wand is safe to use in future. That particular issue will be settled after the spell test.'

Mrs Meany looked like she was about to explode.

'The academy has no money anyway,' continued the High Witch. 'We can't even afford to repair the leaky roof, let alone pay you compensation.'

Mrs Meany glared at Molly. 'I hope you fail,' she hissed.

The High Witch addressed the visitors.

'You will of course be allowed to witness the test. There is a viewing platform at the side of the range.'

The High Witch turned to Molly.

'Miss Miggins, you will present yourself at the spell testing range in twenty minutes.'

Molly picked up Wonky from the desk and pushed him into her secret pocket. Mr Miggins placed his arm round her shoulder and smiled encouragingly.

'You can do this, Molly. Eight out of ten targets is doable.'

Before Molly could reply, the door flew open and Aunt Matilda burst in.

'Hello, Molly, hello everyone, hope I'm not too late.'

The High Witch groaned.

'Good afternoon, Matilda, to what do we owe this unexpected pleasure?'

'I came to speak up for my niece, Molly Miggins, but my car wouldn't start, Wilberforce chewed through the cables again and...'

'Spare me the details, Matilda,' said the High Witch.' You were always late for class when we were at the academy ourselves, nothing has changed, it seems.'

The High Witch led the committee from the room. Ramona Rustbucket closed the door behind them and turned to Molly.

'Twenty minutes,' she reminded her. 'Don't be late.'

Aunt Matilda looked puzzled. 'Twenty minutes?'

'We have to test Wonky on the spell firing range, now he's been straightened, Aunt Matilda,' explained Molly.

Aunt Matilda pulled a handful of cornflakes from her pocket and put them in her bag.

'The spell test range, ooh that's exciting isn't it, Wilberforce? We'll look forward to seeing that.'

Chapter Thirteen

Twenty minutes later Molly stood uncertainly on the
spell testing range as the guests and committee took
their places on the viewing platform, above a pile of
hay bales at the side of the range. Twenty yards in
front of her was a large, dragon-shaped target. Molly
pulled Wonky from her secret pocket and addressed
him.

'Hello, Molly Miggins. Are you ready for the test?'
'I wish we didn't have to do it, Wonky. We're only
allowed two misses.'
'Try to relax,' said Wonky, 'I think we can do this.'
The High Witch rose to her feet, took a
handkerchief from her pocket and held it in the air.
'The targets are controlled by our range controller
up in the tower over there.'
She pointed to a rickety looking shed on top of
four wooden poles. A narrow flight of steps led up to
the control room.
'On my signal, the range controller will set the
targets moving. The targets will get progressively
smaller as the test goes on. The contestant must hit at
least eight of the targets to pass. The hits will be
verified by our spotter. Good luck, Molly Miggins.'
Molly glanced up at the visitors' platform
nervously. Mr Miggins gave her the thumbs up. Aunt
Matilda waved while wriggling her hips in time to the
music on her MP3 player. Mr Havelots sat alongside
a stern looking Mrs Snitcher and an even sterner
looking Mrs Meany. There was no sign of Henrietta.
The High Witch dropped her handkerchief and the
large dragon target began to move slowly to the left.
Molly closed her eyes for a moment then stuck her
tongue out of the corner of her mouth and

concentrated hard. Wonky's face appeared on the wand.

'Good luck, Molly Miggins,' he said.

Molly pointed Wonky towards the dragon and followed the movement of the target.

'*Blast,*' she called.

A red spell shot out of Wonky like a bullet and smashed into the target.

'One,' called a voice from the viewing platform.

Molly grinned and glanced at Wonky. Her smile became a grimace as she noticed that the end of the wand had twisted again.

'It seems the heat from the spell has reversed the repair,' said Wonky sadly. 'I'm back to my old shape.'

Molly gritted her teeth.

'Never mind, Wonky, we can still do this.'

'Wonky nodded.

'Just remember to aim me slightly lower and to the left, Molly Miggins.'

The second target, a cauldron, came into view and trundled slowly along the range.

Molly aimed Wonky just in front of the target and fired.

'*Blast.*'

The spell hit the target, dead centre.

'Two,' called the voice.

Molly's concentrated even harder as the next target, a witch on a broomstick, came into view.

'*Blast,*' called Molly.

The spell hit the top of the witch's hat.

'Three.'

'We were lucky there, Wonky,' whispered Molly.

Target four was a black cat and was quite a lot smaller than the third target. Molly aimed at its front paw and hit it in the middle of its chest.

'Four,' called the spotter.

Molly grinned happily.

'I think we're getting the hang of this, Wonky, you aren't quite as bent as you were before. I'd never have hit that cat yesterday.'

'I think you are right, Molly Miggins, the twist isn't as bad as it was.'

'Target five came down the range, Molly aimed at the owl's right foot, the spell crashed into its left eye.'

'Five.'

Molly glanced up at the platform. Her father grinned and waved. Aunt Matilda had vanished.

As target six came into view Molly noticed a familiar figure climbing the stair to the tower.

'What's Henrietta up to?' she muttered.

Molly blasted target six, a full sized witch's hat, on its brim.

'Six,' called the voice from the viewing platform.

Target seven was a spell book. Molly hit it on the page number, at the very bottom.

'Seven.'

'Phew,' she said.' Only three more to go, Wonky.'

Molly waited for target eight, but nothing arrived. Then a bat target shot across the range in front of her. Before she could blink it hit the end of the run and reversed back towards the start.

Molly looked towards the platform for guidance. The High Witch motioned for her to continue.

Molly waited for the bat to return, she lined up Wonky and followed the fast moving target across the skyline.

'*Blast,*' she called.

The spell flew under the bat, missing it by inches.

'Miss,' called the spotter.

'Bother,' said Molly.

Molly willed herself to concentrate as her hands began to shake.

Target nine was a small moon. Molly watched it carefully as it careered across in front of her, just as Molly cast her spell, the target stopped dead.

'Miss,' called the voice.

'This is so unfair,' cried Molly.

Molly looked over towards the tower and waited for the final target to appear. To her surprise she saw Aunt Matilda climb the rickety wooden staircase. A few seconds later there was a bright flash, then the tenth target, a life sized mouse, hurtled across the range.

Molly tried to follow the target but was put off by the sound of shouting from the control tower. She looked up to see Henrietta run down the steps screaming at the top of her voice, a few steps behind came a man in brown overalls, behind him came a rat, the size of a dog, by the time it reached the bottom of the stair it was the size of a pony. It sniffed the air as it turned towards the viewing gallery. When it moved again it was the size of an elephant.

Aunt Matilda staggered groggily down the stairs.

'Wilberforce,' she called. 'Come to Mummy, there's a good boy.'

'Give him some cornflakes, Auntie,' called Molly.

'None left,' shouted Aunt Matilda. 'That girl was cheating,' she added.

Wilberforce had grown to the size of a double-decker bus. He plodded across the grass towards the viewing platform and eyed its occupants menacingly. The High Witch raised her wand and fired a spell at the rat. It hit Wilberforce on the ear. Wilberforce twitched his whiskers, sniffed the air and moved forward.

Aunt Matilda fired a shrink spell and hit Wilberforce on the back but it had no effect, the rat continued to grow. By the time he reached the viewing platform he was the size of a house.

Wilberforce crashed into the platform sending its occupants flying through the air. Mrs Meany fell awkwardly and sprained her ankle. She got up and tried to limp away but was soon caught by Wilberforce.

Mrs Meany screamed as Wilberforce picked her up in his claws and held her in front of his nose. He sniffed at her twice, then dropped her onto the hay bales below. Mrs Meany grabbed for her bag of shopping and tried to crawl away but Wilberforce placed his paw on the bag and sniffed at it excitedly.

Mrs Meany let go and edged away on her bottom. Wilberforce tore open the plastic bag with his claws and pulled out a box of cornflakes.

Molly was transfixed, then a voice from behind brought her back to her senses. She turned to see Granny Whitewand holding a weeping Henrietta by the ear.

'Use the birthday spell I gave you, Millie,' she called.

Molly pulled the scrap of parchment from her pocket, aimed Wonky at Wilberforce and read the spell backwards.

'WON EM TISISSA!'

A purple spell came out of Wonky and spread out like a huge cloud, engulfing Wilberforce. As it cleared, Molly saw Mrs Meany sitting on the floor with her head in her hands.

'Oh my, oh my,' she muttered, over and over.

Mr Miggins helped Mr Havelots to his feet as the High Witch and committee members climbed out of the rubble of the viewing platform and dusted themselves down. Wilberforce was nowhere to be seen.

The High Witch pulled a splinter of wood from her tunic and announced that the spell test was over.

'The hearing will resume in the committee room in fifteen minutes,' she said.

Molly turned to see Aunt Matilda march Henrietta back towards the academy, her fingers pinching the young girl's ear. She patted her bag with her free hand as she walked.

'Good boy, Wilberforce,' she said.

Chapter Fourteen

'The committee would like to thank Molly Miggins for saving the viewing party from the jaws of that vile creature,' said the High Witch.

'He isn't vile, he...' began Aunt Matilda.

'I think we'd all like to thank Molly,' interrupted Mr Miggins. He gave Aunt Matilda a warning look and nodded towards her bag. Aunt Matilda pushed Wilberforce's head back inside and fastened it up quickly.

'Mr Havelots, the committee would like an explanation for Henrietta's behaviour today. What was she doing in the control tower without permission?'

'I just wanted to see how it worked,' said Henrietta, 'that's all.'

The High Witch called the control tower operator.

'Mr Lever, can you shed any light on the mystery. What on earth happened up there?'

Mr Lever cleared his throat and read from a notepad.

'I was going about my business, controlling the targets, when this young lady (he pointed at Henrietta) appeared in the control booth. She informed me that the High Witch had sent instructions to make the task more difficult for the contestant and advised me to speed up the process. As this was an extremely unusual request, I went to the intercom to check that the new instructions were correct. As soon as I turned my back, she took control of the targets. When I told her to leave them alone she pointed her wand at me. I wasn't going to take any chances with that, I mean, I didn't fancy being turned into a toad or something, so I went back to the intercom and told them to get a message to the High Witch at once.'

Mr Havelots got to his feet.

'If Henrietta said that she had instructions, then...'

'Henrietta received no such instructions from me, Mr Havelots,' said the High Witch. 'Do go on Mr Lever.'

'Well,' said the controller. 'The next thing I know, this lady, (he nodded towards Aunt Matilda) came into the tower and pulled out her wand. She told the youngster to get away from the controls. The youngster refused, pointed her wand at the lady and cast a spell at her. There was a flash from her wand that seemed to strike the lady's bag. The next thing I know there was a rat as big as a cat in the tower and it got bigger, right in front of my eyes. The young lady panicked and ran for the door. I wasn't far behind her, I can tell you.'

Mr Havelots turned to Henrietta. 'Really darling, that wasn't very nice.'

Mrs Meany glared at Mr Havelots.

'I want compensation,' she said. 'I was in shock when that rat grabbed me.'

'So do I,' said Mrs Snitcher. 'I was in shock too.'

The High Witch clapped her hands and called for order.

'Has anyone anything to add before the committee makes its final recommendation?' she asked.

'Molly didn't pass the test,' shouted Henrietta. 'She only hit seven targets.'

'I only got a chance at nine,' replied Molly. 'We would have hit that last one. I had my eye in by then.'

'The test was cancelled because of circumstance beyond the control of the contestant,' said the High Witch.

She looked down her long nose at Molly.

'Place the wand on the table, please, Miss Miggins.'

Molly laid Wonky on the table with trembling hands and sat down again.

'It seems to me,' said the High Witch. 'That the wand has reverted back to its original shape and the attempted repair has been unsuccessful.'

The committee members nodded their heads in agreement.

'Burn it then,' hissed Mrs Snitcher.

'But Wonky saved Mrs Meany,' cried Molly.

'Burn it, burn it,' chanted Henrietta.

Granny Whitewand got slowly to her feet.

'Burn the wand and you burn our own history,' she said.

'What's this?' asked the High Witch. 'Do we have new evidence to consider?'

'In Mrs Miggins' absence, I've been doing some research in the academy library,' said the old witch. 'It appears that there is a lot more to Molly's wand than first meets the eye.'

Granny Whitewand hobbled to the front of the room and placed a pile of papers and parchments on the table.

'Look for yourself,' she said. 'The markings on Wonky are identical to the description of a wand that all witch kind holds in the highest esteem. If you send this wand to the incinerator you will be destroying the most famous wand ever made. Wonky, is Cedron, the saviour of the White Academy.'

The High Witch was nonplussed.

'Ced..Ced..Cedron?' she stuttered.

'There's the proof,' said Granny Whitewand, as she pointed to the pile of documents. 'Remember our history? Cedron was almost burnt out after the twenty-four hour spell cast. After he fired his last spell to bring down Morgana, he was left blackened and twisted and almost consumed by the heat. Griselda herself wrote an account of the spell cast and described Cedron very clearly. She also drew a detailed picture of him in her book. Compare her drawing to the one I made of Wonky, you will find they are identical.'

The High Witch sat down, dumbfounded.

'We gave away our prize possession to a novice witch. How can this have happened?'

'We must take him back,' said Ramona Rustbucket. 'He must be put on display, in a place of honour at the academy.'

'He's mine,' said Molly. 'I want him back.'

'I'll give you fifty thousand pounds for him,' said Mr Havelots, 'no, wait, one hundred thousand.'

'You can't sell him,' cried Molly.

'Buy him, Dad,' Henrietta encouraged. 'You can't let poor people keep something so valuable.'

'Half a million pounds,' yelled Mr Havelots.

The High Witch sat down and stared blankly at the far wall.

'Half a million pounds,' she muttered.

'Imagine what we could do with that?' said one of the committee members. 'New roof, computers, a new kitchen...'

Ramona Rustbucket was shocked.

'This is the mighty Cedron, were it not for his bravery the Black Academy would have been victorious and we would not be here today. We cannot sell this wand.'

Aunt Matilda was equally outraged.

'The very idea,' she said.

Granny Whitewand got to her unsteady feet again and straightened up as far as her bent back allowed.

'You are also forgetting one other simple, but important point. Wonky/Cedron, and Molly have bonded. You cannot easily break that bond unless the wand, or witch, agrees to it.'

The High Witch stood up and placed both hands on the table. She looked either side to the committee members, then to Molly.

'Granny Whitewand is correct, it is in our constitution. We may only break the bond if the wand is deemed dangerous or the witch incompetent.'

'Both reasons apply in this case,' snarled Mrs Snitcher. 'Burn it.'

'We cannot, and will not, burn this wand,' said the High Witch. 'I would personally like to see it placed in the display cabinet in the great hall of the academy. Legend has it that it was displayed there for centuries until it was lost.'

'One million pounds,' said Mr Havelots.

The High Witch swallowed deeply.

'It really is a most generous offer, Mr Havelots, but it isn't just a decision for the academy any more. We have to hear what Molly and Wonk...I mean, Cedron, have to say.'

Molly got nervously to her feet and looked round the room.

'I don't want to give up Wonky. He's the best wand a witch could ask for. He's not just my wand. He's become my friend too. I wouldn't want to swap him for anything else.'

'Selfish girl,' hissed a committee member. 'Think of the academy.'

'I need him to help me get Mum back,' said Molly stubbornly. 'Wonky knows what we need to do on Thursday night, when we re-run the vanishing trick.'

'Then hand him over on Friday.'

'I don't want to hand him over at all,' said Molly. 'Wonky is mine and I want to keep him.'

'One million pounds to the academy and half a million pounds to the Miggins family,' said Mr Havelots.'

'It is a very generous offer,' said Mr Miggins. 'But Wonky is Molly's wand and wands are very personal things. Wonky can no longer be classed as dangerous. He isn't as badly twisted now as he was before the repair, Molly's test spells on the range prove that. She will have to work hard at controlling him, but I'm sure she will succeed in that. At the end of the day it's her choice. Molly is my daughter, I love her very much and if she wants to keep Wonky, then all the money in the world wouldn't be enough to make me try to persuade her to give him up.'

'Don't listen, Dad,' said Henrietta, 'I want that wand. Why should *she* have it?'

'I'll buy the wand and donate it to the academy,' said Mr Havelots. 'You could put him in the glass display case with a Havelots sponsors logo above it. Everyone wins then.'

'Consider very carefully, Molly Miggins,' said the High Witch. 'Half a million pounds could buy you anything you wanted.'

'It can't buy another Wonky,' said Molly, 'he's a one-off.'

The High Witch began to argue but was silenced by a deep voice from the back of the room.

'A task has been set and the task will be fulfilled or failed,' said the voice.

Molly turned around to see the wizard she had met at the fairground the night her mum and dad disappeared. The High Witch became flustered. It wasn't often a wizard from the Magic Council paid a visit.

'Your Excellency,' she said. 'We were just discussing what to do about this wand.'

'I heard most of the discussion,' said the wizard. 'And I have to say I was shocked by a lot of it.'

The High Witch blushed and busied herself with the papers on the table.

'We've only just discovered the identity of the wand,' she said. 'Should such a valuable treasure be entrusted to so lowly a witch?'

'The wand was given deliberately,' replied the wizard. 'The Council has high hopes for Molly Miggins.'

'We bow to your authority,' blustered the High Witch, wondering what Molly had done to deserve such confidence.

'Let the wand speak and put an end to this,' said the wizard. 'It will be Cedron's choice.'

The wizard turned to Molly and smiled.

'Address your wand, Molly, let us hear what he has to say.'

Molly picked up Wonky from the table and concentrated hard. Wonky's fat little face appeared on the wand. The High Witch and committee members bowed.

'Oh Mighty, Cedron, the gathering wishes to hear your valued opinion on this matter of grave importance. The academy wishes you to return to them, the novice witch wishes to keep you. We have agreed that the decision will be yours. Please give us the benefit of your wisdom.'

Wonky smiled softly.

'I have listened to the debate and there is good reasoning in both arguments. Before I announce my decision I would like to explain a thing or two.

After the spell cast I was just about finished as a wand. I was literally, burnt out. Griselda tried to repair me but I was too weak to respond. She made a gift of me to the academy and I was placed on display in the glass cabinet in the entrance hall. I didn't mind at all, I was glad of the rest.

I lay there, undisturbed for two hundred years. Then, as now, the academy building was in great need of repair. Funds were raised and the work started in the entrance hall. I was put in a case and placed in the vault with all the other valuables.

A year or so later, a witch, called Martha, discovered me when the vault was being spring cleaned and took me home, to show her mother.

The mother was angry with her daughter and told her to take me back immediately. She ran the risk of being thrown out of the academy. Unfortunately for Martha, when she returned to the academy in the morning, the vault was locked and there was no way of sneaking me back in. She decided to hide me on the top shelf of the wand room and there I lay, undiscovered, for a further one hundred and twenty years. I had more or less recovered by then and I was getting very lonely.

During that time, the academy suffered a fire and the vault was destroyed. The academy naturally assumed that I had perished in the fire, so no search was ever made and no one ever looked for me.

Then, about thirty years ago a new wand master arrived, a certain Mr Grimtoad. He was a young man back then and was determined to run his department efficiently. He had the wand room cleaned out and new shelves were put in place. It was during this process that I was discovered again.

Mr Grimtoad took me for an old, lost wand and kept me in reserve in case a spare wand was needed at short notice. Occasionally I was offered to a novice witch, but I was always sent back within a few days after some mishap or other.

On Saturday, I was given to a young witch called Molly Miggins. I knew she was different to the rest from the very start. We got along famously despite our first spell going awry. Molly Miggins is kind, patient, trusting and respectful, she will be a credit to this academy. She accepted me without question, despite my disability and she has defended me throughout this trial, even taking the blame for my failings.

I have to admit that the thought of lying on a soft cushion in an air conditioned cabinet, does have a certain appeal. I am old and I had got used to the idea of retirement. That was of course, before I met Molly Miggins. When I'm with her I feel young again. She is vibrant, enthusiastic, she makes me feel wanted, which is a very nice feeling. I also have to say that the steam treatment I received today worked wonders on my old joints.

I was Cedron, but that was a dozen lifetimes ago. I am now known as Wonky and while that name may not be as grand, or revered, as my former one, I am happy with it. It suits me.

So, in answer to your question, I choose to stay with my friend, Molly Miggins.'

The wizard nodded sagely.

'I think you have made a very wise decision, Wonky. Let all here now witness, that the wand formally known as Cedron, will, in future, be known as Wonky and is bonded for life to the novice witch, Molly Miggins.'

Molly grinned a huge grin and waved Wonky in the air. Granny Whitewand and Aunt Matilda danced a little jig. Even Mrs Meany wiped away a tear.

The celebrations were cut short by Henrietta. She had sat in silence during Wonky's speech, but now she could no longer hide her frustration.

'That wand should be mine,' she hissed. 'I will have it.'

Henrietta darted forward and snatched Wonky from Molly's hand. She pointed it at the High Witch and laughed evilly.

'Don't try to take this from me or I'll blast you,' she said. 'This wand should be mine. It's far too valuable for a nobody like her. I'll look after it from now on.'

Molly leapt toward Henrietta and tried to grab Wonky, but Henrietta stepped back and held Wonky out of reach.

'I did warn you,' she sneered.

Henrietta pointed Wonky at the middle of Molly's face.

I found the very spell for you in the *Witchit*,' she said. 'Are you ready to wear a chicken's face?'

'Don't try it, Henrietta,' warned Molly, 'it's not your wand.'

Henrietta ignored her.

'Chicken face,' she called.

There was a flash of brilliant light, followed by a deafening bang. When the spell mist cleared, Molly found herself holding Wonky. There was no sign of Henrietta.

Half an hour later, the High Witch led Molly and her family back through the narrow passageways to the entrance hall.

'You are a very lucky young witch to be given such a treasure, Molly Miggins. Make sure you look after it.'

'I will,' said Molly happily. 'Our first challenge is to get my mum back from Gloop.'

'What's Gloop?' asked the High Witch.

'I'm not sure yet, but I have a feeling I'm going to find out very soon,' said Molly.

As they walked through the hall the High Witch pointed out the painting of Griselda, Wonky's first and only other proper owner. Molly stood in front of the painting for a while, then addressed Wonky to show him the portrait.

'I hope I turn out to be half the witch she was, Wonky,' said Molly.

'You can never be the same as her, Molly Miggins, you are quite different. It may be that you turn out to be an even better witch than the great Griselda. Only time will tell. We have a long journey ahead of us and I cannot wait for it to begin. I have a feeling that life is about to become exciting again.'

Molly smiled.

'What happened to Henrietta?' she said. 'I hope she's not hurt.'

'Henrietta wanted to be the centre of attention and now she is,' said Wonky. 'Look in the glass cabinet.'

Molly walked to the centre of the hall. Henrietta was sitting in the display cabinet. Her face was black with soot; her hair was a mess of tangles. She banged on the glass as Molly approached.

'Let me out of here, NOW! I'll get you for this, Molly Miggins.'

Chapter Fifteen

Thursday passed slowly. Molly went to school and handed in her lines. All the teachers commented on how well presented they were. Molly bit her tongue and said nothing about the quill spell.

Henrietta wasn't present at the morning witchcraft lesson but all the class had heard about the events at the academy. Even Desdemona Dark was impressed.

Molly went to see the head teacher and handed her a letter, signed by the High Witch, stating that not only was Wonky safe, but that Molly was to be encouraged in every way possible as she was on a fast track course set out by the Magic Council.

By ten o'clock Molly was convinced that it was lunchtime. At lunch she thought it must be time to go home. Sally and Jenny came over to sit with her on the playground steps.

'Mum got me tickets for the show tonight,' said Sally. 'I can't wait, wish your dad good luck from me.'

'Same from me,' said Jenny. 'We've got tickets too, I'm really excited about it. I'm sure Mr Miggins will bring your mum home tonight, Molly.'

'If time goes much slower, it will stop completely,' moaned Molly.

Simon Snitcher walked over to the girls and stood in front of the steps.

'Are there any tickets left for the show tonight?' he asked.

'Sorry, they're sold out,' said Jenny.

Simon pulled a face.

'No one told me that your dad was going to try the vanishing act again. I missed it last time too,' he moaned.

'So, you want to be there tonight because you hope the trick will go wrong again. That's not very nice is it?' said Sally.

'Henrietta's family have a private box to watch from,' said Simon. 'I might ask her if I can join them.'

'I think we can guess the answer to that one,' laughed Jenny.

Simon became grumpy.

'You are causing a hazard, sitting there,' he said.

'GO AWAY SIMON!' said the three girls in unison.

'I'll report you,' he threatened, but walked off anyway.

Two minutes later Malcolm Meany wandered over.

'How much are the tickets for tonight?' he asked.

'Ten pounds for adults, five for children and OAPs, but there are none left,' said Molly.

'Oh, I've got the tickets,' said Malcolm. 'We got free ones from your father as part of the compensation. I was thinking about selling one that's all.'

'Simon's desperate for a ticket,' whispered Sally. 'He was asking us if there were any left.'

'Was he? That's cool, we've got one spare. I'll see if he wants to buy it.'

'But you got it for free,' said Molly. 'You should give it away or have a raffle or something among your friends, really.'

'Great idea,' said Malcolm.

He fished his calculator from his bag and did some quick working out.

'Twenty tickets at 50p is ten pounds. Not bad for a five pound ticket,' he gloated.

Malcolm skipped away calling to Simon.

'Hey, Simon, did I hear you're looking for a ticket for the show tonight?'

Molly shook her head in disbelief.

'That's awful,' she said. 'Simon is supposed to be his best friend.'

'Money is Malcolm's best friend,' said Jenny. 'Always has been, always will be.'

Sally said goodbye as her mother's car pulled up at the side of the school.

'It's time to go back to my own school. See you tonight, Molly. I'll meet you in the foyer.'

*****

They reached the theatre at six forty-five. Mr Miggins showed Granny Whitewand to her seat then went backstage to sort out his special effects while Molly and Mrs McCraggity bought sweets and drinks in the foyer. Molly popped a minty ball in her mouth and studied the audience as they arrived through the main door. All the junior witches were allowed to wear their outfits when they attended a magic performance. Molly saw plenty of them dotted about the place.

Sally Slowspell spotted Molly as soon as she entered the building and ran across to greet her.

'Hello Molly, I bet you're excited. I am, and it's not even my mum that's going to be rescued.'

Molly smiled nervously. 'I hope it all goes to plan' she said. 'Dad's found an old spell that might help.'

Molly motioned for Sally to move closer, then whispered in her ear. 'I might get to help out later.'

'That's great,' whispered Sally, 'but why are we whispering?'

'Because Henrietta Havelots has just come in and I want her to think we have a secret,' said Molly. 'She's not wearing her witch's uniform either.'

Sally stole a glance over her shoulder, then turned back and whispered in Molly's ear.

'I think she's fallen for it. She's stretching her neck trying to see what we are up to. Isn't it a rule that junior witches have to wear their costumes at magic events?'

'Henrietta makes her own rules,' said Molly. 'I like wearing my new clothes.'

'Oh, I know what I meant to ask,' said Sally. 'Did you try the cabinet?'

'Yes, but it didn't work,' said Molly. 'I got stuck in some green, slimy stuff. If Dad's spell doesn't work tonight, I'll have another go.'

Molly's best friend, Jenny, arrived with her brother and parents. Molly waved to her and she walked over to join them.

'You two look great in your uniforms. I want to be a witch, it's not fair,' she complained.

Molly told her about Henrietta and how she paid to join the academy.

Jenny was angry. 'That makes it even worse. I wish I was rich.'

'Then you might be like Henrietta and we wouldn't be friends,' said Molly. 'Anyway, you can help me when I do my spells. If you learn enough you might get to be a scholar-sponsor thing.'

'Can anyone be a scholar-sponsor thing?' Jenny asked,

'Think so,' said Molly. 'If Henrietta can do it, others must be able to as well.'

'I'll talk to Mum.' Jenny was a lot happier.

At seven fifteen they moved through to their seats. The girls had a really good view from a box overlooking the stage. Molly sat with Jenny and Sally on either side. Granny Whitewand snored away gently in her seat at the end of the row.

The warm up act was a clown called Jasper Japes. He tried to do all sorts of magic tricks but got them all wrong. Then he tried juggling but the clubs kept landing on his head when he threw them in the air. Molly and her friends thought he was hilarious and all three had tears running down their faces.

At eight o'clock the announcer came on to introduce the 'The Great Rudolpho'. The audience all stood as they clapped and cheered him onto the stage. Molly looked around proudly. In the box opposite she spotted Henrietta Havelots with her family. She stared at Molly with crossed eyes and pulled a face. Molly thumbed her nose, stuck out her tongue and turned back to the stage.

The Great Rudolpho started off with a vanishing card trick and followed it up by producing a huge beach ball out of thin air. He then asked for a volunteer from the audience and made everyone laugh when he smashed the man's watch up in a hanky, before sending him back to his seat. Then he asked the man's wife to check under her hat. The watch was there, as good as new.

Half an hour later there was a break and everyone went to the bar for drinks. Molly stood with her friends in the children's area drinking fizzy pop. Sally groaned as she saw Henrietta approach them with a smug look on her face.

'I've been given a backstage pass,' she boasted. 'I can watch the last part of the show from the wings.'

Molly wasn't impressed.

'I've seen all the tricks close up anyway, I could probably do some of them myself,' she scoffed. 'I don't need a back stage pass. I may be *on* the stage a little later.'

'With the clown act,' said Henrietta nastily.

She skipped away waving her pass in the air.

Chapter Sixteen

After the interval they all returned to their seats.
There was a dance act on stage. Sally was fascinated
by the light show. Molly knew how the lights worked
from helping her father and pointed up to the metal
frame, high above their heads.

'That's the lighting rig,' she said. 'It's got all
different coloured lights on it. They control them
from a computer down there.' Molly pointed to a
small area in front of the stage. A man was standing
in front of a computer screen, pressing keys on a large
keyboard.

'Wow,' said Sally enviously, 'I'd love to have a go
at that.'

Molly offered to ask her dad.

'He might be able to fix it for a rehearsal, or
something.'

The Great Rudolpho returned to the stage amidst
more thunderous applause.

'Ladies and Gentlemen, Boys and Girls, I give
you, the Magic Rabbit Trick.'

Molly crossed her fingers and hoped the rabbits
behaved themselves.

The trick worked perfectly and the audience sat in
amazement as they watched the rabbits pop out of the
magician's sleeve and disappear into his top hat.
Afterwards, Mr Miggins went through his normal
routine, pulling snakes out of pockets and turning cats
into bats. The crowd sat, open mouthed, as he made a
bar of chocolate turn into a real penguin. After
another half hour he reached the climax of the act.

'Tonight, I'd like to ask for the assistance of a very
special member of the audience.'

He looked up into the box where Molly was sitting.

'My own daughter, and newly appointed junior witch, Molly Miggins.'

The audience all turned to look at Molly. She stood nervously as they began to chant her name.

'Molly, Molly, Molly.'

She slipped out of the box and ran down the stairs. A man was waiting for her and opened the door that led through to the stage.

'Wait in the wings until he calls you on,' he said. 'Good luck.'

Molly walked to the curtain at the side of the stage; her father was at the front talking to the audience while stage hands moved things about. They pushed a big trunk into the centre of the stage and a large cabinet was set up just behind it. Molly recognised it as the cabinet her mum had disappeared in.

Molly heard a noise behind her and turned to see Henrietta Havelots leaning against a pillar.

'I'm going on stage,' said Molly happily.

'You don't need a clown suit,' Henrietta goaded. 'You look like one already in that yellow tunic.'

Molly decided to ignore her and turned her attention to the stage. The assistants were still scurrying to and fro, pushing boxes, sliding screens and large mirrors into place.

The magician finished his talk, explained a little about the finale and then introduced Molly.

She walked onto the stage waving to the crowd. Up in the box, Sally and Jenny stood on their seats as they clapped and cheered. Granny Whitewand had woken up at last and let out a piercing whistle.

'Yaaaay, Millie,' she yelled.

When the audience had quietened, the lights dimmed and a thin mist began to cover the stage.

The magician asked for a volunteer from the audience to come on stage to check the equipment and make sure that there were no false doors on the cabinet. A woman stepped up from the front row, but before she could get to the stage, Henrietta ran on from the wings.

'I'll help,' she offered.

Molly rolled her eyes to the ceiling.

Mr Miggins agreed reluctantly.

Henrietta gave a twirl to the crowd to show off her new designer dress and gave Molly one of her looks.

Henrietta strolled around the stage as though she was the star of the show. She made a great deal of fuss over checking the vanishing cabinet. The magician opened the mirrored doors front and back, to show there was no one hiding in it. Then he lifted the lid of the trunk and asked Henrietta to look inside.

'Empty,' she agreed. 'Can you make me vanish? I want to go in the trunk.'

Rudolpho shook his head.

'I think we'll use an object instead of a real person this time,' he said to Henrietta. 'I'm hoping that the spell from the previous performance will reverse and Mrs Miggins will re-appear in the cabinet. We don't want anything to get in the way of that, do we?'

A mumble of agreement went round the audience. There was a call of 'good luck' from the back of the hall.

The magician asked Henrietta to return to her place in the wings.

Henrietta refused.

'I think I'll stay here, if you don't mind.'

'I think I do mind, Henrietta. There will be magic flying around this stage very soon and I wouldn't want you to get hurt,' said Mr Miggins firmly.

Henrietta stamped her foot and began to walk off stage but as soon as the magician turned away to talk to Molly, she leapt behind the vanishing cabinet and squatted down with a big grin on her face.

Henrietta congratulated herself as she realised she hadn't been seen. She was determined that there was only going to be one star of this show and that person wasn't going to be Mrs Miggins.

'I've had an idea, Molly,' said the magician quietly. 'The old spell I was working on this morning, mentions using an item that used to belong to the missing person. If we send it across, it might call your mother to it.'

Molly nodded.

'What do we have of Mum's?'

'You have something, Molly, you have her magic ring. At least it used to be hers. I'm hoping her connection to it is still strong enough to help us.'

Molly slipped the ring from her finger and placed it on the floor of the cabinet. The magician closed the door softly and raised his wand in the air.

Behind the cabinet Henrietta became very excited as she heard talk of a magic ring.

'Why don't I own a magic ring?' she said to herself. 'I should have one.' She narrowed her eyes and thought hard. It wasn't stealing, not really. Dad could always pay them for it later.

Henrietta pulled the catch at the back of the cabinet and tiptoed inside, as she picked up the ring the door clicked shut behind her.

Henrietta examined the ring closely, she wondered how it worked? Was it an invisibility ring or did it grant wishes? Outside she could hear the voice of the magician as he cast his spell.

Henrietta slipped the ring onto her finger just as the blue mist began to form on the floor of the cabinet. She looked around for a door handle to escape from the box but there only seemed to be the one that led to the stage, where she would be discovered with her new found treasure.

Suddenly she felt a tingling in her fingers and ears. The ring expanded and fell to the floor with a '*plink*'. Henrietta stared at her hands, or what used to be her hands. To her horror she found she was looking at two huge flapping fish. Henrietta screamed and turned towards the door. As she did, she caught sight of herself in the mirrored glass. She screamed again as she saw the fish head that was sat on her shoulders.

Henrietta panicked, kicked at the glass and the door swung open onto the stage, Molly and the magician stared open-mouthed as the fish-headed Henrietta flapped around inside the booth. She looked up to see the audience laughing, thinking it was all part of the act. Henrietta covered her fish face with her fish hands and ran screaming through the back of the cabinet into the grey fog.

Mr Havelots was on stage in an instant.

'What have you done to Henrietta? Bring her back this minute.'

Mr Miggins tried to calm the millionaire down.

'The fish head and hands will almost certainly only be temporary, Mr Havelots. As for her disappearance, I think that is more her own fault than anyone else's. I have two hundred witnesses here who heard me tell her to leave the stage.'

Mr Havelots put his head in his hands. 'I know she can be a pain at times, but she's my daughter, please bring her back.'

'If I knew where she was I would do just that,' said Mr Miggins as he opened the trunk. 'Normally she would come out here, but there's something wrong. Don't worry too much, Henrietta will be with Mrs Miggins at the moment, she'll look after her until we find a way to bring them home.'

Mrs Havelots joined her husband on the stage.

'You should go in after her,' she said to Mr Miggins. 'It's your faulty equipment after all.'

Mr Miggins tried to explain his position.

'If I go into the cabinet, who will control the spell from this end?'

The Havelots eyes fell on Molly.

'Molly can do it, she's a witch now.'

'Molly only took her promise a few days ago, Mrs Havelots, but you may have something there,' said Mr Miggins thoughtfully.

The magician turned to Molly.

'Do you think you can handle the spell, Molly? It's quite a powerful one.'

'I tried it the other night, Dad,' whispered Molly behind her hand. It worked, but I got stuck in green goo.'

Mr Miggins looked puzzled.

'Maybe that's the problem, Molly; I really should have a look at it myself. What happened?'

'The back mirror cleared then it turned transparent,' said Molly.

'That's right,' said the magician, 'then what happened?'

'It formed a grey mist. But then a few seconds later it turned into this yucky green slime, I couldn't get through it, Dad.'

Mr Miggins was perplexed.

'I think I really do need to have a look at it Molly. You know the command, are you sure you want to do this? We can wake up Granny Whitewand if you don't.'

'I'll be fine, Dad. Wonky and I will look after things this end.'

'If I'm not back in half an hour, or you have any problem, get Granny Whitewand to help you,' said the magician. He gave Molly a kiss on the forehead.

'I will, Dad. Be careful.'

Mr Miggins entered the cabinet and closed the door behind him.

Molly pulled Wonky from her secret pocket and addressed the wand.

Wonky appeared looking worried.

'Things aren't going too well are they, Molly Miggins?'

'We can handle this, Wonky,' said Molly with more confidence than she felt.

'You aren't going to rely on that old relic I hope,' spluttered Mrs Havelots. 'Surely you have something newer than that?'

Molly ignored the remark and raised Wonky high above her head. Her heart was beating fast; she felt beads of sweat on her forehead. Behind her the audience held its breath.

'Vanish!' she cried.

The spell flew from Wonky and crashed into the mirrored cabinet before reflecting back on itself. The Havelots ducked as it flew over their heads and crashed into the emergency fire exit.

'Oops,' said Molly.

Molly raised Wonky again and aimed at the top of the cabinet. The Havelots lay down on the floor.

'VANISH!'

This time the spell hit the frame of the cabinet, it began to pulsate rhythmically as blue smoke crept from under the door. The audience applauded in relief. The Havelots stood up and brushed dust from their clothes.

Molly watched the cabinet with concern, she was sure it hadn't made that noise before. Molly called up Wonky again and together they walked to the glass door.

The cabinet began to shake violently, Molly stepped back as green ooze began to seep under the door frame.

'Bother, this isn't supposed to happen, Wonky.'

Wonky agreed.

Molly summoned up all her courage and grabbed the handle of the cabinet.

'After three, Wonky, one, two, THREE.'

Molly pulled at the door with all her might, but it would not open. She tried again but the door was sealed shut.

'Bother, bother, bother,' she groaned.

As quickly as it had begun, the cabinet ceased to shake and the humming noise stopped.

Molly pulled on the door handle and it opened with ease. The cabinet was empty apart from a small gold ring on the floor. Molly picked it up and slipped it onto her finger.

'Good luck, Dad,' she whispered.

Molly closed the cabinet door quietly behind her and walked back onto the stage. The audience was silent; the Havelots sat on the big trunk and held hands. Then from the upper circle she heard a single clap. Molly looked up to see Sally Slowspell standing in front of her seat; Jenny joined her and began to clap too. Within seconds the entire audience was on its feet applauding madly.

Molly stood at the centre of the stage, waving Wonky in the air. From the wings she heard a familiar voice.

'Well done, young Millie. Now you've got to keep them happy until your father gets back.'

Chapter Seventeen

After fifteen minutes the audience began to get a little
restless. Molly looked at her watch. Dad said he
needed half an hour. She decided to give them
something to look at while they waited.

She pulled Wonky from her secret pocket, stuck
out her tongue and concentrated hard.

Wonky's face appeared, looking worried.

'Do you think this is a good idea?' he asked.

Molly nodded, 'let's do the mouse trick.'

Molly adjusted her stance and pointed the wand
towards the right end of the stage where there was
plenty of open space.

'Dancing Mouses,' she cried.

The spell shot out from Wonky like a bullet from
a gun. It hit the corner of the stage and bounced up
the aisle between the rows of seats. The crowd turned
their heads as it whooshed between them.

The spell hit the back wall with a bang. A large
grey cloud of smoke appeared which began to drift
back down the aisle. Molly watched with a fixed
smile as out from the cloud came four enormous, pink
hippos dressed in tutu's and ballet shoes. They stood
on their points, linked front legs and danced sideways
down the aisle to the stage.

'Oops,' said Molly.

The audience was delighted.

Molly stared glumly at the hippos as they hopped
onto the stage. They began to dance sideways across
the wooden floor. As they returned to the aisle end
there was a loud *'pop'* and another hippo emerged
from the cloud to join in the ballet.

Molly began to wonder if the stage was strong enough to hold them.

She checked her watch again, the half hour was up.

She turned to the wings to ask Granny Whitewand for help, but she was sat in the director's chair snoring loudly. Molly was worried.

She addressed Wonky. 'What shall I do, Wonky? I think something's gone wrong.'

Wonky nodded. 'Give it a couple of minutes longer?'

Molly checked her watch again and sighed nervously.

'I think we're going to have to go in ourselves, Wonky.'

Wonky thought for a moment and reluctantly agreed. 'I can't see there is anything else we can do, Molly Miggins.'

Molly walked to the wings and gently shook Granny Whitewand's shoulder.

'Hey, what? Get off, dratted bees,' she shouted, waving her hands in the air.

'It's Molly, Grandma, I need your help.'

'It's me that needs help with all these pesky bees,' said Granny Whitewand.

'I have to go into the cabinet, Grandma. Can you cast the spell for me?'

'You wouldn't get me in there,' said the old witch with feeling. 'It's not safe.'

'I still have to go, Grandma. Mum and Dad need me.'

Granny Whitewand yawned, straightened her teeth and followed Molly across to the stage.

'What's with the hippos?' she asked with a puzzled look.

'They were supposed to be mice,' Molly replied.

'Better than bees,' said Granny Whitewand. 'They attack you in your sleep.'

The old witch pointed her wand at the hippos and called up a strange sounding spell. There was a loud flash and one by one the hippos began to explode, leaving five small piles of pink dust on the stage.

The audience began to boo; someone started a slow hand clap.

'Don't worry about them, Millie, I'll set a sleep spell on them in a moment, they won't wake up until I let them.'

She placed a soft hand on Molly's wrist.

'Good luck, Millie,' she said gently, 'you're a very brave young girl.'

Molly didn't feel brave, the only thing she could feel were her knees knocking together. She walked slowly to the vanishing cabinet, trying to think positive thoughts.

'It's now or never, Wonky. I don't think I could do this if I thought about it for too long.'

Granny Whitewand waited until Molly was inside, then she raised her wand above her head.

'See you soon, Grandma,' Molly whispered as she pulled the door shut.

Molly heard Granny Whitewand call the *Vanish* spell and waited as the blue smoke began to swirl around her feet. The rear mirror became transparent, then it began to dissolve into a fine grey mist. Molly took a deep breath and stepped forward into the fog.

*****

Molly made her way to the back of the cabinet, a thin curtain of silver grey mist hung in the air in front of her.

'No green gunk,' said Molly.

'I think you spoke too soon, Molly Miggins,' replied Wonky.

Molly watched, fascinated, as a green puddle formed at her feet. It expanded rapidly and began to climb at an alarming rate until it had completely engulfed the curtain.

Molly held out her hand and softly touched the dripping green wall.

'Yuck,' she said.

She pushed her arm in as far as it would go, but the green film stretched with it. Then she tried making a hole using Wonky, but the curtain just stretched even further.

'Bother,' said Molly.

The green slimy curtain began to solidify.

'We'll have to be quick, Wonky, it's going off.'

'On impulse Molly pushed her ring hand into the thickening wall. To her amazement and delight, it went straight through.

Molly moved her arm in a circular motion and a large tear appeared in the jelly-like wall.

'Quick, Wonky, let's get through before it seals itself up again.'

Molly took a deep breath and climbed into the fast closing tear. There was a sucking noise behind her as she passed through and the green slime wall repaired itself.

Molly found herself in almost total darkness. She took a step forward and tripped over a large stone. The sound echoed through the gloom. She picked herself up and gingerly took another pace forward.

'Mum? Dad?' she called. 'I'm here.'

Chapter Eighteen

Molly held Wonky at arm's length and addressed
him. His friendly little face glowed as it appeared on
the wand.

'I think we need some light, Wonky.'

Molly held the wand above her head and cast the
glow in the dark spell. A thin blue light emanated
from Wonky.

'That's better,' said Molly. 'At least we won't trip
over anything in the dark now.'

She turned to face the curtain. It was sealed.
Molly ran her ring hand over the smooth surface.

'It looks like we're here for a while, Wonky,' said
Molly. 'The curtain only seems to stay open for a
short time. We might have to hang around a bit when
we find Mum.'

Molly looked around. She appeared to be in a
large rock chamber. There was a solid wall to the
right, while a narrow track led away to the left.
Directly in front, a wider path stretched as far as she
could see. The path looked to run uphill; away in the
distance Molly could see a faint green glow.

Molly decided to investigate the left hand path
first. She walked for about twenty-five yards before
she came to another rock wall. Molly turned to the
left, there was another curtain. This one was in solid
form too.

'I think I've worked it out, Wonky,' said Molly
after a short pause. 'Mum would have gone to the
back of the cabinet, through the other curtain back
there, then she would have followed this path, gone
through this curtain and into the trunk on the stage.
The magic spell that Dad casts must open up both
curtains.'

As if to prove her point the curtain began to glow, slowly it became transparent. Molly pushed her head through the clear curtain. Ahead she could see the entrance to one end of the vanishing trunk.

Molly pulled her head back quickly as the transparent film began to turn into a sticky green mess. She thrust her right arm into the gluey substance and the curtain stretched out in front of her. Pulling her arm back she tried her ring hand. After some resistance it passed through the sticky jelly wall.

Molly thought for a moment.

'I can't work out what this green, gunky stuff is, Wonky. I can't see why it would be needed. It only seems to appear after the curtains have been opened for a few seconds. It's all very odd.'

Molly decided that it was a question her father might be able to answer, so she stored it away for later.

As the curtain began to solidify again, Molly turned back to the chamber.

'Right, Wonky,' she said quietly, 'let's see where that other path takes us.'

Molly held Wonky in front of her as she began the climb, solid rock walls lay either side of her and the floor was littered with loose stones. Molly was glad she had Wonky for company.

'I wouldn't like to be in this place on my own, Wonky,' she confided.

Wonky agreed.

After two hundred yards the ground began to even out. The green glow up ahead became stronger. Molly decided she would be able to see without the aid of

Wonky, so she shut him down and slipped him into her pocket.

'It's probably best to keep you a secret for now, Wonky,' she whispered.

Molly trudged on; the light became brighter all the time until she could see everything very clearly.

To the right and left there were small, cave-like rooms cut out of the rock. Each of the rooms had a wide doorway. Molly looked into one or two as she passed by, they were completely empty.

'This gets odder and odder,' whispered Molly to herself.

She walked on; ahead she could see the path divide at a junction. The right path led into darkness, the left path was lit by the strange green glow. Molly followed the light.

She walked slowly along the track, treading carefully to avoid tripping on the loose rocks. Ahead, to the right, she noticed that the door to one of the rooms was pulsating with a sickly green luminance. Molly stepped across to examine it but was brought to a halt by a voice.

'Help, please, help.'

Molly peered into the room. A young boy was standing by a small bed. He rubbed his eyes as though he could scarcely believe what he was seeing. 'Are you a real witch?' he asked.

'Sort of,' said Molly, 'I'm an apprentice witch to be precise. What are you doing down here?'

'You're not with Gloop?' asked the boy suspiciously.

Molly looked around.

'I'm not with anyone, I'm Molly Miggins and I've come to find my mum.'

The boy nodded.

'Ah, I see, did she disappear during a vanishing act by any chance?'

Molly looked puzzled.

'She did actually. Do you know where she is?'

The boy pointed to the right.

'She's probably along there somewhere. I've lost count of how many are in here now. Gloop won't say. He only lets us talk to him, not to each other.'

'This Gloop sounds a nasty piece of work,' said Molly. 'Why don't you just gang up on him? He can't be that tough.'

Suddenly there was a sloppy, squidgy sort of noise from a room further up the path.

'Quick, hide,' said the boy, 'don't let him find you. I'm Ches, by the way.'

Molly ran into the next empty cell and hid in the shadows; outside she heard a deep gurgling voice.

'Goodnight, my friends. Gloop is coming round to tuck you in and tell you a scary bedtime story.'

Molly frowned and wondered why he was trying to talk while drinking a glass of water. She held her breath as a green shadow passed by the doorway. Then she heard the gurgling voice again.

'Chesney! Never fear, Gloop is here. It's time for your nightmare. What shall we talk about tonight? I could tell you all about the headless horseman of Horsley Castle if you like?'

'Go away, Gloop. You don't scare me anymore,' said Chesney.

'That's not fair,' said Gloop. 'What did I ever do to un-scare you?'

'Just being yourself, Gloop. If it wasn't for the force field on the door, I'd be out of here and so would the rest of them.'

Gloop laughed a liquid laugh. 'My green electroplasm will ensure that never happens, Chesney. Now would you like the headless horseman or a nice poem?'

Chesney groaned.

'Give me the horseman, anything but the poetry.'

Gloop laughed again. Molly thought he sounded just like a sink emptying.

As Gloop began his story, Molly crept out of the cell and tiptoed along the pathway. There were green lit cells dotted about on both sides of the track; in each one a person was either lying on a low bed or sitting at a small table. She slipped by unnoticed.

Molly counted as she went, casting a quick look into each room. There were twenty-seven lit cells but none of them held her mother. Dad was here somewhere too. Molly began to think he must have got lost taking the dark path at the junction.

Molly began to feel dejected. It had all become too difficult.

'Bother,' she said, louder than she meant to.

Off to the left, she heard a voice call quietly.

'Molly? Molly Miggins? I'm here, Molly.'

'Mum!' Molly exclaimed and ran towards the voice.

'Shhhh, you must be quiet, Molly, don't let Gloop hear you.'

Molly found herself turning a sharp corner that she hadn't noticed before. On the left was a cell, slightly larger than the others, in the doorway just behind the pulsating green door, stood Mrs Miggins. She held her finger to her lips and shushed at Molly. She pointed to the cell opposite. Molly peered in and saw her father snoring quietly on a long, low bed.

Molly crept back to her mum; she felt tears welling up in her eyes. She tried to speak but a huge lump appeared in her throat.

Mrs Miggins smiled fondly, then became serious.

'Molly, listen carefully,' she whispered. 'Be very careful, Gloop is more dangerous than he looks. He keeps us here by way of these screens. We can't get through them. I may have been able to had I had my wand, but I didn't have it with me when I came through the curtain. Dad left his on the trunk on stage.'

She stopped and listened for a moment, the drone of Gloop's voice drifted up from Chesney's cell.

'It's fine; he'll be another fifteen minutes at least yet, he's already been here tonight. Now, let me have a good look at you.'

Molly did a twirl.

'My, my, Molly, don't you look a picture. That yellow tunic is incredible, and that hat is fabulous. I take it the Witches Promise passed off without a hitch?'

'Sort of,' said Molly, remembering the hat and the crystal ball. 'I did have to... No, that's probably best left for now. How can I get you out?'

Mrs Miggins shook her head.

'I really don't know, Molly. We get let out of these cells for twenty minutes at a time, if we need the bathroom, that's about it. He brings food round in the morning, it's always tinned stuff, he must have a store down here somewhere. After that he spends the day in his chill room. It re-energises him.'

The witch leant forward and whispered.

'Molly, listen to me. Gloop is always around and about through the night. It's his time. You must find somewhere to hide until tomorrow. We can talk properly then, when he's resting.'

Molly looked around; there was an empty cell about twenty feet away.

'I'll hide in there for now, Mum. There's a dark passageway at the junction a bit further down the track, I'll head for that when he's telling someone else their bedtime story.'

Mrs Miggins looked at her daughter with pride.

'Be careful, Molly; don't let him get too close, he can send you to sleep.'

Molly tiptoed to the end cell and sat in the shadows. She still hadn't seen this Gloop person and she needed a plan. Molly closed her eyes to think; a few seconds later she was fast asleep.

Molly woke to the familiar whine of Henrietta Havelot's voice; she seemed very close by. Molly crept to the doorway and peered out. Henrietta was in the next cell along, on the opposite side.

Molly could see Henrietta clearly, but Gloop was in the corner of the cell hidden from view.

'My father will have you in court for this,' Henrietta threatened.

Gloop laughed his watery laugh. 'I don't think you'll find a lawyer down here, my girl.'

'Look,' said Henrietta, changing tack. 'My father is very rich, VERY RICH,' she added slowly. 'He'll give you lots of money if you send me back. Never mind the rest of them, you can keep them forever. Just let me go, you'll be the richest ghost in the world.'

'I have all I need here, Henrietta,' said Gloop happily. 'I have you and my other friends, I wouldn't swop you for money.'

Henrietta began to cry.

'I want my mum, I miss my dad, I miss my pony and my jewellery and my nice clothes,' she stamped her foot. 'Let me go this minute you jellied freak!'

'Don't say such things,' said Gloop sadly. 'You'll get to like it here, everyone does.'

Molly began to ease her way back into her hiding place, as she crawled she knelt on a pebble.

'OW!'

Henrietta looked across and spotted Molly.

Molly put her finger to her lips in a desperate plea for Henrietta to be quiet.

'Molly Miggins, get me out of here at once, it's your fault I'm here in the first place.'

'Bother,' said Molly under her breath. 'That's torn it.'

Molly decided to make a run for it and managed to get past Henrietta's cell before a surprised Gloop came out.

'What have we here?' he chuckled wetly.

Molly tried to run, but felt an overpowering urge to lie down and sleep, she fought it and made an extra few yards before weariness engulfed her. As she drifted off to sleep she felt herself being carried in the cold, sticky arms of Gloop.

Chapter Nineteen

Molly woke up to find a pair of huge, limpid eyes staring down at her from a green jelly head. She recoiled instinctively. Molly's reaction seemed to please the owner of the head, his face split into a huge grin.

'Scary, aren't I?' he said.

'I suppose so,' said Molly, rubbing her eyes. 'Especially when someone thinks they've just woken up from a bad dream only to find they are still in it.'

'Bad dreams are great aren't they?' agreed the green head. 'I'm Gloop and I'm pleased to make your acquaintance.'

Gloop held out a wobbly green hand. Molly shook it gingerly.

'I'm Molly Miggins,' said Molly, 'I've come to take my mum home.'

'Ah, Miggins, I thought that was the name I heard. That would be your mum over there in cell 124.'

'Probably' said Molly, who had no idea what number her mum's cell was.

'She's a very friendly lady.' said Gloop with a smile. He looked around to check that he wasn't being overheard. 'She's one of my favourites; she gets extra spaghetti for breakfast.'

'Spaghetti?' Molly was aghast; 'I have Wheaty Flakes with cold milk. Mum usually has boiled eggs.'

Gloop nodded.

'Yes, she told me that, two soft boiled eggs with toast soldiers, it does sound nice. Unfortunately I can't get fresh stuff. I did manage to get hold of a few thousand tins of spaghetti though. You'll get used to it, everyone does.'

Gloop stood up and began to pace the room, his green body quivering as he walked.

'I'm sorry, but I can't let you go home, Molly Miggins. I'd like to, I really would, but if I let you go, I'd have to let everyone go and then I'd be alone and I don't want to go through that again.'

Gloop made his wobbly way to a small table that was set in the centre of the cell. He sat on the floor and pulled out a small stool.

'Come and sit with me, let's have a chat,' he said cheerily, 'ask me anything you like.'

Molly sat on the stool, rested her elbows on the table and cupped her chin in her hands.

'What... *who,* are you?' said asked.

Gloop puffed out his jelly chest.

'I'm Gloop, the scariest ghost that ever existed.'

'You don't look very scary; you look like you've just come out of the fridge.'

'I am very scary, believe me,' said Gloop pulling what he hoped was a scary face.

'You look like a rather large, lime jelly that's just come out of the mould,' replied Molly.

She stuck a finger into Gloop's squishy tummy and examined it before putting it in her mouth.

'Yuck, you don't taste like lime jelly,' said Molly with a disgusted look.

'You see?' said Gloop, 'scary *and* uneatable.'

Molly wasn't impressed.

'You stink a bit too, you smell like you've gone off.'

'All ghosts smell a bit,' agreed Gloop. 'It adds to the scariness and I can be very scary.'

'Go on then,' urged Molly. 'Be scary.'

Gloop became silent for a moment; suddenly he lurched forward until his face was only inches away from Molly's. His large, jelly head expanded to twice the size. Gloop put his fingers into his mouth and pulled sideways, making it look like a wobbly, green letterbox. He rolled his eyes into the back of his head and lolled out his slimy tongue, green gunk dripped all over the table.

'Wow,' said Molly. 'That was impressive.'

'Told you,' said Gloop, 'I could out-scare a scarecrow.'

'Scarecrows aren't very scary really,' said Molly.

'They are to crows,' said Gloop, that's why they're called...'

'Scarecrows, yes I do see, but people aren't scared of them are they?'

'They would be if they had sharp teeth and long claws, and chased them round the field with a hatchet,' argued Gloop.

'I suppose they would be in that case,' agreed Molly.

'There you are then,' said Gloop. 'They're scary, and I'm a lot scarier than them.'

Molly agreed that he probably was.

'There's one thing been puzzling me,' said Molly. 'How come you're made of jelly? Most ghosts are just made of...not much.'

'It was an accident,' said Gloop sadly.

'Do tell,' said Molly.

'I was once a normal ghost, the sort that appears on long staircases and sticks their head through closed doors. I used to haunt the old castle with a few friends. We were very good at it; they used to send TV crews there to try to film us. They never could of course, as soon as they unloaded their equipment, we used to nip over to the manor house and haunt that for a while instead. They only had one ghost over there usually, *Dreadful Doris*, they called her. She was dreadful too, at haunting, she wouldn't say boo to a goose.'

Gloop sat quietly for a while, lost in his thoughts. Molly cleared her throat.

'Ahem.'

'Sorry, where was I? Oh yes, I know.'

Gloop leant back against the table leg and crossed his jelly feet.

'I got a bit bored at the castle; it was the same thing every night. We'd clanked a few chains and frightened a few visitors by popping out of paintings, the usual stuff. Then I heard about a job going at the theatre. Old *Wailing Will* managed to get himself stuck in a bottle and got thrown into the recycle lorry. So I decided to give it a try over there. It was great to start with; I used to scare the stage hands and some of the actors by popping up behind them when they were putting their make-up on.'

'The jelly?' Molly reminded him.

'Well,' said Gloop, not in the least bit put out. 'I decided to scare the kitchen staff one day. They were preparing for a big after-show party. They made trifles and sausage rolls, all sorts of stuff. I decided that I was going to give them a big surprise by popping out of the cake when they tried to cut it. So I hid in the fridge and waited for them to put it in there. They didn't, they put a huge green jelly mould in there instead, so I thought, okay, that'll do. I hid in the jelly thinking I'd be out in an hour or two, but they shut the door on Tuesday night and no one came back until Friday morning; by then I was stuck.'

Molly tried not to laugh.

'Anyway, to make a long story even longer,' continued Gloop, 'they finally carried me out and set me on a long table with all the other food. I thought I was going to be eaten alive. But the lights warmed me up a bit and I managed to slide off the table, I was beginning to turn into a jelly puddle. I needed somewhere to hide while I thought about what to do next, so I slid under the door of what I thought was an old cupboard. It turned out to be a vanishing cabinet and that afternoon they tested it for the evening matinee. I ended up here all alone, I couldn't get back; no matter how hard I tried. I had to make this place my home, but it got very lonely after a while.'

'So you decided to capture people?' said Molly, 'that isn't very nice.'

'It's better than being alone for years and years,' said Gloop. 'You should try it.'

Molly began to feel very sorry for Gloop.

'Wouldn't you rather be back with your friends, haunting the castle?' she asked.

'I'd do anything to go back there,' said Gloop wistfully. 'But it isn't going to happen, so we'll have to make the most of it here. Gloop has new friends now.'

Molly decided to get more information while she could.

'How do you control the yucky film on the cells?'

'I've got secret switches,' whispered Gloop, looking around to make sure no one was listening. 'The whole place runs on electroplasm; I invented it,' he boasted.

'Electro what?' said Molly.

'Plasm, It's a good word isn't it? Basically it's bits of me mixed in with the static electrickery that comes through the curtain from the outside. I can regenerate in my chilly room during the day, so when I need it, I scrape off bits of jelly from my tummy or my backside and put a bit of electrickery into it. The electrickery is very important, without it you just get a green puddle on the floor, but when you add it, well, you can see the results.'

'It's very good,' agreed Molly. 'I bet no one can get through that.'

'I can,' said Gloop, happily. 'But then I invented it.'

Molly opened her mouth to ask another question, but Gloop had turned away.

'Goodnight, Molly Miggins, I have work to do now, I haven't given John at number forty-two his bedtime nightmare yet.'

Gloop waved, then passed through the green film whistling a watery tune.

Molly sat for a while and thought about things. Rescuing Mum and Dad was one thing, but there were twenty-seven others, twenty-eight if you included Henrietta. Molly was sorely tempted not to include her after the part she played in getting her caught.

She decided to take her mother's advice and wait until morning. Gloop would be resting then; anyway, she was tired, it had been a long day.

Molly called goodnight to her parent's and lay back on the small cot; she was asleep within seconds.

Chapter Twenty

Molly was awakened by the sound of watery whistling. She rubbed her eyes twice before she remembered why she wasn't waking up in her own bed at home.

Gloop stood at the table and poured cold spaghetti from a tin onto a plastic plate.

'Rise and shine, Molly Miggins. It's time for breakfast.'

'Thank you,' said Molly limply. She never had liked spaghetti that much. 'I don't suppose you have beans instead?' she asked.

'I think there are some beans back there,' he said thoughtfully. 'But they are under a couple of thousand tins of spaghetti, so I can't get at them, sorry.'

Gloop left Molly to eat her breakfast and moved on to the next cell.

Molly looked at the cold orange mess on the plate and decided she wasn't hungry. She sat by the table and waited until Gloop's cheerful voice became fainter as he began serving breakfast to the captives down the hill.

Molly pushed her ring hand through the green film and made a large hole. She climbed through quickly and tiptoed past Henrietta's cell. She needn't have worried; Henrietta was asleep on her cot, sucking on a thumb.

Molly crept to her mother's cell.

Mrs Miggins was astonished to see her daughter. She called to Mr Miggins in a low voice. Molly's father was equally impressed.

'How did you escape, Molly?'

'My magic ring can get through the green stuff,' said Molly, 'look.'

Molly pushed her arm into her mother's cell. Mrs Miggins took Molly's hand and squeezed it tightly.

'Clever girl. Do you have a plan?'

'Not really,' said Molly, 'I'm going to have a look around while Gloop is handing out breakfast. Where's his chill room?'

Molly's mother pointed to the right.

'His chill room is at the end of this row, Molly. The bathrooms are next door to it. I think the doors are on an automatic switch of some kind. If any of us needs the bathroom we just press the button on the wall here.' The force field clears and we can go outside, it seems to works for four of us at a time. There are four bathrooms up there. We get fifteen minutes and then a bell rings and it's time to come back.'

'Why don't the four of you who are out just make a run for it?' asked Molly.

'Because he seals off the passageway just below the last occupied cell when he's regenerating. We can't escape.'

Molly turned and crept to the end of the passage. There were five closed doors, Molly tried them in turn. The first four were very basic bathrooms consisting of a hole in the floor and a bucket of lukewarm water. Molly shuddered and told herself never to complain about the shower water being cold, ever again.

The final door led to Gloop's chill room. The door was activated and Molly had to use her ring to gain access. She shivered as soon as she stepped inside. The cell was lit with the usual green glow. Icicles hung from the ceiling and in one corner was a huge block of ice.

Molly turned to face the other wall. There was a long bank of switches with numbers above each one. At the end was a huge metal lever with the words On and Off written on the wall in chalk. Molly looked along the line of switches until she found number 124. She flicked it up and ran back outside. Mrs Miggins was standing outside her cell waiting for her.

'Well done, Molly,' she whispered. 'Now switch it back on and go back to your cell, we'll have to wait until Gloop takes his re-energising nap before we make our escape.'

*****

Molly crept back into her cell just as Henrietta woke up.

'Gloop, get me some runny eggs and soldiers now! You can't expect me to eat this...slop.'

Molly heard the sound of a plastic plate being thrown against a wall.

'Wait until my father hears about this. You're dead meat, Gloop.'

'He's already been dead for years, Henrietta,' Molly called. 'He's hardly likely to be scared by that.'

'And just who asked you for your opinion, Molly Miggins?' Henrietta paused, then went on. 'Your whole family are useless, you're all supposed to practice magic, yet you're all trapped in here. Maybe if you actually used magic instead of practicing it one of you might get us out of here.'

Molly began to get annoyed.

'Just think about this, Henrietta, if one of us does manage to free ourselves, who do you think will be the last person we bother to release? Maybe there's one person that might even get left behind to keep Gloop company.'

'You wouldn't dare,' said Henrietta angrily. If you have a plan you had better include me in it or my father will have you in gaol.'

'We could just say we didn't know you were here,' said Molly with a grin.

'Don't you dare do that, Molly Miggins, take me with you, please, I'll be your friend forever, I'll...I'll...I'll give you my Zeppo wand.'

'I like my own wand thank you,' said Molly patting her secret pocket.

Half an hour later Gloop returned with his breakfast trolley.

'Good day, my friends,' he gargled. 'Gloop is off to regenerate, the bathrooms are now available.'

Molly waited until her screen was opened for the bathroom break before leaving her cell. She didn't want Gloop to come out unexpectedly and find her in the passage when the force field on her door was still in place.

Molly wandered up to the bathrooms with three other girls. They walked in a group whispering among themselves, one of them turned to Molly.

'You're new aren't you?'

'Yes, I'm Molly Miggins, I've come to get my mum.'

'I'm Holly. Are you a real witch?'

'Sort of,' said Molly. 'I'm just learning.'

'I'd love to be a witch,' said Holly, 'I'd soon sort Gloop out then.'

They passed Henrietta's cell as they talked.

'If you can do magic you could get us out of here, we miss our families,' said Holly sadly.

'It's all right for her, she's got her family with her,' shouted Henrietta. 'Don't trust her; it's her fault I'm here.'

'Ignore her,' Molly told the girls, 'she's just used to getting everything her own way.'

Holly laughed.

'She's only been here a few hours and we haven't heard her shut up yet.'

'She's consistent,' said Molly. 'She's just the same at school.'

Molly washed her face in the clean water bucket and waited for the bell before wandering back to her cell. The water was warm. Molly assumed it was a result of Gloop's electrickery, though she couldn't see a boiler or a heater anywhere.

She was tempted to put her plan into action immediately, but fought off the impulse. She decided it would be better to let the usual, daily routine get under way before they attempted an escape.

Half an hour later Molly's father appeared at her cell door.

'Hello, Molly. I'm sorry I wasn't able to rescue Mum for you. I've just been talking to her and she's told me everything. Thank goodness you had your magic ring.'

'It's okay, now we're all together,' said Molly brightly. 'I wasn't expecting to find all these people here.'

Mr Miggins nodded.

'It was a big surprise to me too. Gloop got me with his sleep spell while I was talking to Mum. It's going to be difficult isn't it? I don't think we can leave all these poor people behind. I just wish I had my wand with me, I might have been able to help you.'

'I have a plan, Dad. I think it has a good chance of working. I have Wonky with me and Granny Whitewand is controlling the cabinet. If she can stay awake that is. She's having trouble with bees.'

'Ah, the bees are back are they?' said Mr Miggins with a smile. 'She's had a lot of trouble with them.'

Molly pushed her ring hand out of her cell and tore a hole in the green film. As she stepped out into the corridor her father crouched down and gave her a big hug.

'Right,' said Mr Miggins after short while, 'it's time for action. I'm in your hands, Molly, what would you like me to do?'

'Stand by with a bucket of warm water,' said Molly. 'Just in case he catches me in his chill room.'

Mr Miggins went into the bathroom and reappeared holding a large plastic bucket.

'If Gloop follows me out, throw it over him,' said Molly. 'That ought to slow him down a bit, he needs to stay cold.'

Molly pushed her ring hand into the green jelly door and made a hole just big enough to climb through. She heard it slurp back together as she stepped into Gloop's bedroom.

Gloop was in the corner, lying on the lump of ice, his eyes fixed on the ceiling.

Molly tiptoed along the wall flicking switches as she went. She could hear the mumble of voices behind her in the passages as she turned off the force fields.

Henrietta's voice was loudest of all. She called out as the freed captives passed by her cell.

'Where are you going? Don't forget me. Hey, let me out too, don't you dare go without me.'

Molly's finger hovered over switch 125, Henrietta's cell. 'No,' she said to herself, 'that would make me as bad as her.' She flicked the switch and heard Henrietta squeal in excitement, then her voice dropped to her usual whine.

'Get out of my way, I'm first.'

Molly reached to the end of the row of switches and turned back towards the doorway leaving only Gloop's door, turned on. As she was about to climb through the screen, her father held up his hand.

'Wait! The force field at the end of the passage is still running, Molly. There must be another switch somewhere, no one can get out until it's turned off, everyone is heading down there.'

Molly looked around. Gloop was still staring at the icicles on the ceiling. Molly checked the switches again but there was only Gloop's cell in the ON position.

'It must be that big lever,' she said to herself.

Molly tiptoed along the line of switches for the second time. She placed two hands on the lever and pulled downwards as gently as she could. There was a quiet click, then a siren sounded and a bright green light began to flash on and off.

Chapter Twenty One

Molly ran for it as Gloop climbed off his ice block. She raced through the door shouting as she ran. 'Now, Dad, let him have it.'

Mr Miggins threw the water straight at Gloop as he arrived in the doorway.

Gloop screamed as the warm water splashed into his face and began to trickle down his quivering, jelly body. He tried to run but his pace slowed as his body began to melt.

Molly hared down the passageway bumping into people as she ran. The lights had all gone out, people called to each other in the darkness.

Molly pulled Wonky from her secret pocket and addressed him.

'Glow in the dark,' she called.

Wonky lit up with a bright blue light. Molly held him above her head and led the throng of captives along the narrow passageway and down the slope. The grey curtain was closed as they approached. Molly hoped that Granny Whitewand was still in the theatre looking after things.

'Please, Grandma,' she whispered under her breath, 'stay awake.'

Holly and her friends pushed their way to the front of the crowd.

'Will we all go through to the same place or will we go back to where we came in?' she asked.

'The spell will send you back from where you came,' Mr Miggins replied. 'Molly, my wife and I will go back to our theatre, you will all go back to the places from which you vanished.'

Molly split the group into two and sent half to the other screen. The grey wall began to vibrate gently.

Gradually a light mist began to form as the wall became transparent.

The crowd became excited and began to cheer. People shook hands and wished each other luck. Then, from the back, came a shout of alarm.

'It's Gloop, he's coming!'

Molly stared at the curtain willing it to become fully clear. Henrietta pushed her way to the front and glared at Molly.

'Wait until my father hears about the way I've been treated.'

Molly gave her a withering look and held Wonky aloft as she walked back through the crowd. She could see a pool of green slime no more than twenty feet away oozing its way down the slope.

'Stand back,' she called, 'don't let that stuff touch you.'

The crowd edged back until they were up against the wall. Gloop oozed closer, Molly turned to check the curtain, it was almost clear.

'Get ready to go,' she called. 'I'll try to hold off Gloop.'

Henrietta became impatient and pushed her hand into the still clearing screen, there was a loud crackling sound as a dozen bright, yellow sparks flew into the air, Molly watched in horror as one of them landed in the centre of the green ooze. There was a flash and loud squelch, suddenly Gloop stood before them.

'I'm afraid I can't allow you to leave, Molly Miggins,' he said wetly. 'I don't want to be alone again.'

'Come with us, Gloop,' Molly said. 'You have your friends in the big house.'

Gloop's eyes dropped.

'They wouldn't want me looking like this, Molly Miggins. I couldn't do my job properly. I'm very sorry but you will have to say here.'

'Molly checked over her shoulder, the curtain was almost clear. She turned back quickly as Gloop slid forward, his arms outstretched. Molly took a step back; Mr Miggins tried to get between his daughter and Gloop.

'I'll stay with you Gloop, let Molly go,' he said.

Gloop shook his head. 'Molly Miggins must stay; she's my best friend now.'

Gloop stared hard at Molly, she began to feel tired, her eyes became heavy. She stifled a yawn as her chin dropped to her chest.

Mr Miggins shook Molly by the shoulders.

'Fight it, Molly, fight it.'

Molly tried to concentrate on Wonky, his face appeared on the wand.

'Think hard, Molly Miggins, think hard.'

Wonky's voice was replaced by Gloop's.

'Sleep Molly Miggins, you are very tired, sleep now,'

Molly began to give in to Gloop's persuasive tone, her arms fell to her side and the grip on Wonky became loose. Then, just as she was about to drift off to sleep she heard a familiar voice in her mind.

'Use your Birthday spell, Millie.'

Molly's head snapped back, her eyes opened wide. She pulled Granny Whitewand's spell from her pocket and held it close to her face.

Remembering her grandmother's instructions, Molly read backwards from the old parchment.

'WON EM TSISSA'

Everything froze in an instant, the murmur of the crowd faded, Gloop stood still, his arms raised, ready to engulf Molly. A deep voice echoed around the chamber.

'What will you have me do?'

Molly stuck out her tongue and concentrated harder than she had ever done in her life as she passed her instructions to the spell.

The deep voice boomed.

'So be it.'

Molly's head cleared and things began to move again. The spell flashed a brilliant white light and hit Gloop right in the middle of his grinning face. His whole body became rigid as he turned to a block of green ice.

Silence filled the chamber. Molly stepped forward and bought Wonky down with all her force on the frozen body of Gloop. There was a loud cracking sound as Gloop smashed into a thousand pieces. As the fragments of ice fell to the floor, a white ghostly shape with the faintest hint of green, drifted up into the air. Gloop circled above the waiting crowd howling happily.

'Goodbye my friends,' he called as he whooshed towards the clearing curtain. There was a flash and a zap as he entered the mist alongside the crawling figure of Henrietta Havelots who could make herself wait no longer.

The grey mist curtain finally cleared completely and one by one Gloop's former prisoners said their goodbyes and walked back to freedom. Mr and Mrs Miggins waited until everyone had gone before they each took hold of one of Molly's hands and entered the swirling mist together.

Chapter Twenty Two

Mrs Miggins stepped out onto the stage to a thunderous round of applause. Mr Miggins followed, with his arms out wide. Molly came out last, waving Wonky in the air. Granny Whitewand shuffled across the stage to stand with the rest of her family.

'Just woke them up,' she whispered. 'They're in for a shock when they find out they've lost a day. I locked the Havelots in the trunk, they were too much trouble.'

Mr Miggins opened the trunk to find Mr and Mrs Havelots still fast asleep.

'I think we'll leave them there for now.' said the magician. 'Whatever happened to Henrietta? She came through before anyone else.'

Molly looked around; there was no sign of her.

The audience quietened as the announcer took to the stage.

'Ladies and Gentlemen, Boys and Girls,' he boomed. 'I think you will all agree that tonight's show has been quite a spectacular event.'

The audience agreed and cheered.

'I would like to thank The Great Rudolpho for a fabulous evening, and I'm sure you will all agree that it is wonderful to have Mrs Miggins back amongst us. But, there was only one real star of the show tonight. Ladies and Gentlemen, Boys and Girls, I give you, our very own, MAGIC MOLLY!'

Molly stepped forward to the front of the stage. She held Wonky high in the air and waved happily. Jenny and Sally stood on their seats and shouted her name as they clapped.

'Molly, Molly.'

Molly's smile became even bigger as she saw the ghostly figure of Gloop flying across the back of the hall. The audience looked up as he flew over their heads. Gloop pulled a scary face as he swooped down low.

'Goodbye, Molly Miggins,' he called. 'Thank you for everything.'

Gloop flew round in a figure of eight then disappeared up the air conditioning outlet.

'Goodbye, Gloop,' whispered Molly. 'Happy haunting.'

Molly bowed and curtseyed until her knees ached. Then Mr and Mrs Miggins stepped forward and they stood as a group for one final bow. As the curtain came down for the last time Molly thought she saw something move on the lighting rig. She told her father about it when they were in the wings.

'I'm sure I saw something move up there,' she said in a puzzled voice.

As the audience left the theatre wondering why they were in broad daylight, Mr Miggins strolled to the front of the stage and looked up at the rig. There, in the centre, behind the big spotlight, was Henrietta Havelots. Her designer dress was torn and dirty. Her face was layered with black soot. Her hair was tangled and covered in green slime.

'Get me down,' she whimpered. 'Please?'

Mr and Mrs Havelots climbed out of the trunk, rubbed their eyes and looked up at the rig in horror.

'We'll get you down in a moment, darling, don't panic.'

'GET ME DOWN!' Henrietta demanded. She looked to where a grinning junior witch stood watching.

'I'LL GET YOU FOR THIS MOLLY MIGGINS.'

The End

4578385R00085

Printed in Great Britain
by Amazon.co.uk, Ltd.,
Marston Gate.